WINSLOW'S PROMISE

WINSLOW'S PROMISE

A Mystery

Eugenia Koukounas

Full Court Press
Englewood Cliffs, New Jersey

Published in the United States of America
by Full Court Press, 601 Palisade Avenue,
Englewood Cliffs, NJ 07632
fullcourtpress.com

ISBN 978-1-946989-44-4
Library of Congress Control No. 2021921962

Editing and book design by Barry Sheinkopf

THIS BOOK IS FOR

My husband, Barry Sheinkopf

AND FOR

Kristos and Foster Perry,

who told me so

ACKNOWLEDGMENTS

I'd like to thank the following people, who read or listened to this book, for their support and technical observations that helped shape it: Kalli Koukounas, Natalie Beaumont, Larry Kaiser, Ray Boswell, Chris Kanka, Sam Gronner, Gail Larkin, Susan Rosenbluth, Lynne Marotta, Tony Wiersielis, Rita Kornfeld, Richard Donatone, Ed Dollinger, and Jim Gold.

A special thanks to George Beck and John "Wheels" for technical advice about police procedure. And to my husband Barry Sheinkopf, who as my editor never fails to say the right thing.

This book was inspired by a moment in "Barbed Wire and Brown Skulls," one of the deeply human tales in Loren Eiseley's *The Night Country*. Two young people come to him with box containing a human skull. Their uncle, an upstanding lawyer in the community, has recently died and left a substantial fortune to the family, who have found the skull among his remains. Eiseley says it's much easier to give such a find to an archaeology department than to bury it and risk untold awkwardness should it somehow be unearthed, or go to the police, who would immediately consider the possibility of foul play. Well, I asked myself, what *would* happen if you went to the police with a disembodied skull? *Winslow's Promise* is my answer to that question.

CHAPTER 1

S ILENCE HOVERS OVER A PARLOR bathed in the flat gray light of an overcast afternoon until the chink-chink of teacups meeting saucers mercifully fills the void. Annie Clairmont, along with her mother Ismene, have just returned from a two-week visit to the family's summer home in Cape Cod. Ginny Spencer had asked that her ashes be scattered there on the property. It had been her favorite place to visit for decades.

It had come as a shock to the entire family that Aunt Ginny left everything to Annie. True, she *had* moved in and nursed her great-aunt through hospice, and while growing up she had spent more time there than anyone else, but it'd stung her cousin Margie Singleton to be overlooked. Only to appear polite, Margie says, "It must have been empty up there in mid-September."

"Mmh," Annie agrees. "My favorite time of year to be there, except maybe January. I love that clear sky in January."

"Did it rain in Dennis like it did here for the last two weeks?"

"We had a break in the weather for a couple of days. Long

enough to scatter her remains in sunshine."

Eyeing the collection of Spode in the curio cabinet next to her, Margie's huge eyes narrow as she considers the effect of her statement before uttering it. "Good luck taking care of all these dust collectors!" Her feline jaw tenses and relaxes a couple of times.

Her brother, whose loose red polo shirt hides a former track star's body, exclaims, "*Margie!*"

"Why?" she snaps, fingering a needlepoint pillow covered in faded violets. "It's no wonder Aunt Ginny left everything to Annie. Only she could appreciate this—"

"Junk?" Annie exhales. Looking out the double window, she spots two squirrels chasing each other across a low branch of an old maple. The tree has stood there for nearly a hundred years, shading the Victorian house. "I never thought so. It was always a second home to me. You never seemed to care about it quite the same way when we visited as kids."

"Goodness!" Margie swipes her bangs off her forehead and tosses her brown hair off her shoulders. "How many times can you listen to the same stories over and over again?"

Annie has decided to go through with her lie, knowing her great-aunt would ultimately forgive her. "Aunt Ginny told me that she wanted you to have this." She pushes a black velvet box across the mahogany coffee table in front of her cousin.

Margie opens it, and her heart-shaped face softens some as she slips the ring onto her finger.

Jim, all elbows and knees, glances dubiously at his cousin. He pushes aside the plate of lemon slices and grabs the last chocolate chip cookie, making it perfectly clear as he bites into it that he doesn't approve of the ruse even if it is for the sake of appeasing his sister.

The platinum ring is shaped like a Russian crown, with a small diamond perched on top. Diamond chips run down the sides of each rib. Margie sniffs, not sure whether she should be pleased. "So old-fashioned." Studying her hand, she murmurs, "Though it's definitely one of her better pieces."

"It looks great on you, since you've got those long fingers—and none of your friends will have anything like it."

"I suppose it's a good conversation piece." Reassured, Margie finally smiles. "Still, that everything was left to *you* is quite a surprise, even if you did spend all that time with her at the end."

Annie does not reply but waits. Margie shrugs, grudgingly admitting to herself that it was Annie who attended Aunt Ginny with real devotion for months, rarely leaving her side. She can't stay angry at Annie for very long anyway. They grew up bickering more like sisters than cousins. And she knows in her heart that Annie's feelings for their great-aunt ran deeper than those of all the other first cousins who dutifully visited Aunt Ginny now and again.

Annie opens two other small boxes, each containing cufflinks that belonged to Aunt Ginny's father. One pair are plain gold squares, the other ovals of silver with mother-of-pearl centers. "I polished the silver for you, knowing you wouldn't bother to."

Jim quickly shoves the rest of the cookie into his mouth and wipes the crumbs from his hands on his khakis before accepting them. "Not exactly conversation pieces with my crowd, but very much appreciated." He tucks them into the pocket of his jacket. Rubbing his shorn head, he winks. "Thanks, Mouse." It's Annie's family nickname.

At this moment, Ismene reappears with a silver tray containing a fresh pot of tea hiding under a cat-shaped tea cozy, and more of the cookies she often bakes just in case anyone drops by. Red hair perfectly coiffed, pulled back in a knot at the nape of her slender neck, she is decked out in a light-gray sweater set and charcoal skirt that show her trim figure to its advantage. The snickerdoodles and chocolate chip cookies are arranged on a plate of Bavarian origin, complete with cabbage roses peeking out from just beyond the edges of the treats. For Ismene, the right plate means God is in the details, and therefore, everything falls into place just so. That is, if one has been graced with any breeding whatsoever, which in turn makes guests as comfortable as possible. Annie, when asked to plate anything, invariably chooses the wrong one, with either too much or too little surface showing—a judgment call measured in millimeters.

Spotting her aunt's engagement ring on her favorite niece's hand, she sets the tray down on the coffee table, lips compressed as she clears away the empty cookie plate. Then she sinks onto the blue wingback, the one that's strategically placed in the center of the room. "Everyone expected after Bill died that, in time. . .but it never happened." Shaking her head as if to rid herself of some thought, she continues, "Is it really possible to have one true love? She was young enough, with plenty of opportunity to start over."

Having received no answer to this question from any of the twenty-something-year-olds sitting around her, Ismene pours lapsang into her cup, nearly spilling it. Taking a sip to give her enough time to recover her self-possession, she muses, "Someone with an absurd sense of sentimentality ought to wear that ring."

Before the silence congeals yet again, Annie explains, "Mom wants me to sell the house. The roof is leaking, the boiler probably needs fixing if not an outright replacement, and the kitchen is so '40s it's practically *au courant*. But I love this home—always have." She has to wait no more than a few seconds before her mother makes her announcement.

"This is far too big for a young single woman to live in alone. So I am moving in with Annie." Casting a glance at her daughter, she adds, "Don't slump over—you know it's not attractive," prompting the young woman to burrow even deeper into the second of the matched wingbacks, the one positioned closer to the corner of the room. "I'd constantly be worried about whether Annie was capable of managing such a large place. Anyway, the condo I moved into is just *too* depressing. People are either very old or so young they walk around wearing baseball caps all the time. The young men pretend to look like athletes, and the women pretend to look like men. Suits or sweats. Whatever happened to trousers, cardigans, skirts, dresses?" She sips her tea. "And don't get me started on what those women look like when they try to wear a dress." She rolls her eyes. "An orangutan in a house dress has more elegance."

Jim, used to his aunt's outrageous observations, turns to his cousin to ask, "This is *good* news?"

"Oh, yeah." Annie returns his skeptical query with a deadpan face. "It's much too empty here without Aunt Ginny."

CROSS-LEGGED ON THE WINDOW SEAT THE NEXT DAY, Annie is listening to the incessant rain, the prospect of what to do next with her life weighing upon her. Unlike her cousins, who find the lure of success that the business world can offer after completing an MBA far more agreeable than she does, she hasn't a clue what she'd like to do with the rest of her life and asks herself jokingly—butcher, baker, candlestick maker? Inspecting the garden below her, she gazes at the huge oak, grown so large that its branches are close enough to the house to be able to climb in and out of certain windows undetected, a feat she and Margie performed once or twice in the past on a dare. She listens as the leaves rustle in the breeze, whispering their long-held secrets. Along the fence, white pines provide privacy from the properties abutting her great-aunt's. She hears the neighbor's dog barking wildly and turns her attention toward the commotion. Out of the corner of her eye, she catches an unexpected movement under the holly bushes. A red fox emerges from beneath one of them, looks up to meet her gaze, staring for what seems a very long time before retreating into the shadow of the pines, her three kits following close behind.

This has been, and still is, Annie's room—her aunt's gift, another world filled with grown-up things that allowed her to imagine all kinds of heroine roles beyond her humdrum daily life of school and, well, more school. Pale green walls, a red Bokhara, a tapestry-covered *fauteuil*, became jumbled up with the scent of honeysuckle creeping up the garden wall in the summertime and Aunt Ginny's perfume—gardenia—in winter, which is now her favorite scent.

"*Annie!*" Her mother's voice slices through her reverie. "Please come down here this moment." She quickly appraises her face in the mirror. Good bones, she thinks, and while it's been two years since she played up her looks—a ruse to keep the wrong kind of attention at bay—perhaps it is time for a new shade of lipstick. Running her hands through her short chestnut curls and straightening her favorite green sweatshirt over a faded blue shirt, she bounds down the stairs.

By the kitchen table stands Mr. Rudy Handelman, her across-the-street neighbor, looking very pleased to see his pink roses occupy center stage on the kitchen table as he murmurs, "No, please, not necessary." The tall robust man in tweeds, cheeks flushed the same color as the flowers, continues, "I wouldn't want to put you out."

Annie, however, once she has echoed her mother's invitation, notices how, for a rather big man, he quickly eases himself into the chair next to Ismene.

"I've for so long admired that lovely stand of forsythia you have on your front lawn, Mr. Handelman. Such a healthy plant," drawls Ismene as Annie pours lemonade into three tall glasses. "How I miss my garden." A sigh escapes her before she adds, "I'm so envious."

"The garden was your Aunt Ginny's greatest joy. The trees, the shrubs, the flowers, are a circle of love she coaxed forth around a fine old home."

Annie smiles. "I remember Auntie digging about, asking me to help her with this or that. I wish I'd paid more attention."

Mr. Handelman nods. "Miss Ginny invited all those whom she loved to take part in her magical garden. I've had the privilege to have spent time here—" suddenly, he blushes at the admission, clearing his throat to continue— "that is, as a boy. I will gladly show you how to take care of this garden. My opportunity to return the favor to your aunt for helping me find my life-long pursuit." Annie shoots the gentleman a grateful look.

Ismene, not liking where the conversation is going, interrupts. "Houses require hard work to keep up, and this one is no exception. I've warned my daughter, *but. . .*she insists." Decreasing the decibel level of her voice to a stage whisper, she confides, "You know, they never listen." Glancing at her daughter, she asks, "Bring some cookies over, darling. No, not that one, take the blue dish instead." She smiles encouragement for her daughter's hosting efforts.

When Annie again takes her seat, she allows the tartness of the lemonade to roll around her tongue as she waits out her mother's Oscar performance.

"Now, Mr. Handelman, I want to take advantage of your knowledgeable experience of this town, having lived here all your life. We have this awful leak in the upstairs study. With the heavy rains we've had for the past weeks, I am afraid that what was once barely a damp spot is now positively ready to come down any moment. Can you recommend anyone to come look at the problem?"

"Dear lady, I know just the person."

Ismene arches one eyebrow to head off any objection her daughter is about to make.

Taking another sip of lemonade, Annie settles into the ladderback chair, scowling at her mother, and grumbles to no one in particular, "You *hated* gardening when I was growing up."

MR. HANDELMAN'S NEPHEW REMAINS ABSOLUTELY STILL as his uncle introduces him. Struck by the young man's economy of movement and piecing blue eyes, Annie misses most of what his uncle is saying. Her reverie is interrupted when the young man clears his throat and sticks out his rough hand to say, "Andrew Rourke. Pleased to meet you." She, who loathes tepid handshakes as a hallmark of the well-bred, returns his firm grip.

"We didn't mean for your uncle to take you away from your work," Ismene says.

He shifts his weight easily on the balls of his feet to face the older woman. "Not a bother, ma'am. You're not far from some stops I have to make—people wanting estimates." He surreptitiously glances at Annie, who hasn't bothered to introduce herself and asks Ismene, "What's the problem?"

Before she can answer, Annie coolly does: "*My* roof is leaking," she says, emphasizing the possessive. "At least I think so, since a corner of the ceiling in the study is soaked."

Ismene studies her nails.

His ears turn red. "Sorry. I assumed. . . ."

"Let me show you." Annie clips on ahead of him, leaving their elders in the palaver hut to discuss matters of greater importance.

The smallest of the four bedrooms was long ago turned into a repository for books, with three of the four walls covered in white built-ins filled with them. A love seat and desk occupy the fourth.

Facing the window that looks onto the backyard is a huge pine desk. The gray tiger cat, Alma, startled from her nap, leaps off the loveseat, covered with cat hairs—proof this is her territory—and ambles past them, muttering protests. A water stain, fanning out from one corner of the ceiling is trickling down toward the window, blistering the yellow paint as it spreads.

"Sounds like the rain's stopped. I saw you've got windows on the third floor, so maybe I take a look from up there. That is—" he faces her, locking eyes— "if you don't mind?"

It's Annie's turn to blush.

She waits on the little bench in the hallway. The last time she sat there was during Aunt Ginny's final days, while the hospice nurse finished up before letting Annie take her place again by the dying woman's side. There was nothing to be done but listen to Aunt

Ginny's labored breath, hoping that, like some human cat, her presence was of comfort. Most of the time, however, Annie had been struck by the thick quiet that hovered over the house during that horrible last week. Once, though, the silence had been shattered by groans coming from her Aunt Ginny, who seemed to be having a nightmare. As Annie tried to gently rouse her to give her some water, the old woman had gasped that it wasn't her fault, that she never meant to cause any harm. When Annie tried to calm her down, all her beloved aunt could do was look away with tears rolling down her eyes. She had refused to speak about it any further.

She hears the contractor rumble down the short flight of stairs before the attic door creaks open. Andrew clears his throat but says nothing. "From the look on your face," she sighs, "it's going to cost a lot more than I hoped."

He gives Annie a hard sideways glance, carefully considers what he will say. "I think you'd better see this for yourself."

With some difficulty, preferring to ignore the young man's caution to be careful and too proud to accept his help, she climbs partially out the windowsill facing the back yard, ducking under one of the larger branches of the oak tree.

Once she steadies herself, one hand grabbing the sill, the other the tree branch, she spots the problem. Her eyes travel the length of the gutter toward the downspout, where most of the water has pooled, and a gasp escapes her lips.

Face down and wedged into the downspout, she sees a human skull.

"How did *that* get there?"

"You tell me."

"Well, I *can't* tell you, because I don't know," she sputters. "I inherited this house a month ago, though I had visited it all my life. I have no idea why it's there."

In one swift movement, he runs his hands through his damp black hair and back again toward his mouth. "Could the, uh, previous owner—"

"Oh, please. Foul play committed by my sick maiden great-aunt . . .it's ridiculous. Anyway, it looks. . .old."

"You an expert?"

"No," she snaps and hesitates a moment before pulling off her sweatshirt. She is about to make her way toward the skull when the young man tries to hold her back. Yanking her arm down to free it from his grasp, she blurts out, "No matter what, it belonged to someone's son. . .or daughter, and attention must be paid."

The roofer shakes his head in disbelief—certainly he knows better, should the law become involved—but her gesture, though absolutely bats, has a deep thoughtfulness running through it that can't be ignored. Taking the sweatshirt from her grasp, he firmly whispers, "I'll do it. Safer." He picks his way toward the edge of the roof, gently wraps the skull in it, and hands it to Annie, noting she isn't a bit squeamish as she ducks back into the attic. He climbs in to find her pulling a handkerchief from her jean pocket to clear the dust and cobwebs from the seat of an old rocker before setting it down.

Annie only becomes aware that she's been shivering when Andrew has draped his black windbreaker around her shoulders. Grateful, she smiles before fully realizing her predicament. "Oh, God, what do I do now?" she wonders aloud, followed by an even more vexing question, "How do I tell my *mother*?"

CHAPTER 2

J OEY SAMARTINO HAS SHUT THE GATE behind him before
starting his customary stroll, as he's done every workday for
almost two decades. It's 7:30 a.m., and the eight-block walk
to and from borough hall, before heading to his own office,
enables him to, in part, fend off his doctor's warning as well as his
wife's complaints about his panatela. Besides, he's done some of his
best thinking at such times, and he needs to make some decisions.

But after only a few steps he hears, "Hey, Joey," as a neighbor
scurries out his kitchen door and down the side steps.

"How you doin', Paul? Great day after all that rain. Can you
believe it's been pouring like crazy for two whole weeks? I've practically forgotten what a sunny day looks like!"

Paul Demaria, caught off balance by this observation, stops, nods
at the blue sky, and collects his thoughts enough to add, "Yeah, but
rain is good for the grass. Keeps the water bill low, too." Giving the
sky one more dutiful glance, he ploughs right into the heart of the
matter. "You know I hate to complain, you having so many more

important things on your mind."

"Nah, got to have something to think about when I'm smoking one of these." The mayor vaguely waves his cigar in Paul's direction. "Nowadays, this walk is one of the few times I can actually light up a cigar without bothering my wife, who's allergic." He suddenly remembers, and pats his neighbor on the back. "Hey, I hear you're a grandfather now. Congratulations."

Paul, nearly a head shorter than the mayor, who stands six-two, leans back to make eye contact, beaming. "Oh, yeah, thanks, Joey. Seven pounds, four ounces. A baby girl. They named her Emily, and is she a *doll!* Jennifer was in labor for eighteen hours, but she's fine now. They both are." In a fit of uncharacteristic sentiment, Paul observes, "You know, there's just something about babies. They make you feel young and old at the same time." After another moment's contemplation, he adds, "Hard to remember when we was kids playing ball, huh, Joey?"

"What are you talkin' about, Paulie? We're still eighteen." Unable not to glance at their spreading girth, they both laugh.

Sheepishly, Paul begins once more. "Like I said, I hate to bother you and all, but it's just that they used to clean the street here first thing Wednesday morning. Something's happened to the route, and now they don't come until noon, and I'm stuck with two cars in the driveway that's really only wide enough for one car. It's a real tango getting in and out of the driveway."

The mayor replies, "I'll give the department of public works a call and see what can be done."

Shaking hands, they part.

As he makes a mental note to speak to the head of the sanitation about the route change, Joey moves on, wondering how he's going to accommodate Paul here on Oak Street and the new Korean family on Chestnut, too. Adjustments will have to be made.

THE BOROUGH CLERK, JOHN KELLY, IS ALREADY IN HIS OFFICE, waiting for Samartino. The mayor pours himself coffee and sits down across from his hard-won friend, someone he's had to prove himself to, since Kelly has seen mayors come and go for forty years. Ought to be considering retirement soon, too—a sore point that neither wants to bring up.

"That was some meeting last night."

"Yep, livelier than usual." The mayor shifts his bulk as he tries to make himself comfortable.

"Looks like you got yourself some opposition this year."

"Never hurts. Don't want to get stale. Twenty-three years in politics is a long time."

Sipping his coffee, John calculates the amount of bravado he needs to cut through, then offers, "Forty years of civil service is even longer."

They sit in quiet for a moment; John lets his eyes travel across his room, which is covered with photos taken with smiling senators and congressmen as well as plaques from the Knights of Columbus and the Lions. The clerk long ago came to terms with being neither handsome nor vain enough to be in the forefront of politics. But he can read people well. His bald head has become familiar in power-broker huddles at public functions, and his face, while not pretty, remains sought after: He gives good advice and can organize people to get things done. But there have been times, he admits to himself, when he's envied Joey that beautiful head of wavy salt-and-pepper hair.

He tries again to take the temperature of the room. "New breed, though—never seen such no-holds-barred attacks inside the *same* party."

"No," Joey sighs, "they don't grow them like they used to." He grins at John rather wearily. "I suppose you and I are just jealous of all that piss and vinegar."

"Well, I remember when you pretty much ran the town for two years with only one councilman out of six sitting up there from your party."

"No picnic." Joey shrugs. "But we'd all go out for a drink afterwards and leave our differences at the dais. Town didn't suffer for it either."

"I think it's those damn computers," John growls. "No one knows how to treat people anymore. All they do is stare at a screen all day."

". . .Excuse me?"

The men turn to see a slight, rather solemn girl—all eyes—craning to get a better look at them. Annie continues, "I know it's early, and I'm sorry to bother you, but I, uh, need some information."

Joey checks the impulse to say the office is still closed when he notices the dark circles under her hazel eyes and the older redhead, who has taken far more care to present a put-together look and appears to be her mother, fuming behind her. Having a mother to contend with himself, he takes pity. "How can I help you?"

"This is very awkward." Annie yanks at her brown cardigan in an attempt to stall as she fights tears about to spill over onto her cheeks.

"And unnecessary," Ismene snaps, yanking her brown tweed blazer down over her blue cords, a seemingly shared family trait when in distress.

John comes up to the counter too, ready to call for crisis intervention if he needs to. "Are you all right, young lady?"

"Me? Uh, yeah." Annie exhales in one breath, "Oh, there's really no good way to say this, but I couldn't live with myself if I didn't come here. You see—well, my mother obviously disagrees—I'm not quite sure what to do."

"You do nothing," growls Ismene. "What any sane, reasonable person would do is *nothing*. Surely you don't think in our family that. . .that anything *untoward* could possibly happen. Why we've been law-abiding citizens. . .always!"

"Mom!" Annie swings around to meet her mother nose to nose, her red face barely equaling her fury. "We've found a *skull* on the roof, in the downspout to be exact. A *human skull!* This isn't a squirrel. You can't just *forget* about it."

"Well, if it bothers you so much, throw it out."

The mayor, not quite able to believe what he's hearing, exclaims, "Throw out a human skull?"

"Does it need to go out on a special trash day?" Ismene inquires.

ANNIE DRAWS BACK THE WHITE LACE CURTAIN in the parlor to peer at the crowd that has surrounded the two police cars in front of the house. The roar of a motorcycle parts the crowd long enough for Andrew Rourke to hop off and make his way up her steps. She hastily covers the chocolate box from which she has taken a bite out of nearly every piece except the ones filled with jelly, then momentarily considers how many second bites she can sneak in and replace the box before her mother notices.

She answers the doorbell. Ismene disappeared after the police questioned her and was nowhere to be found until they finished their business. Annie is somewhat unnerved to see the roofer standing before her. Helmet balanced against his hip, he gives her a practiced, sidelong glance. "I understand you actually walked up to the mayor and told him about it. That takes a lot of guts."

Resisting another glace at the Russell's box, she bristles. "News travels fast."

"Sometimes. I happen to know a couple of people. Besides, I was asked to make an appearance at the police station this morning to provide a statement about how the skull was found *and* why it was moved once we found it." He gives her a pointed look. Swinging the weight of his body away from the door, he adds, "Look, if this is a bad time—"

"No, please come in. I didn't mean to be rude." She shows him to the parlor and adds, "Thank you for taking the time to see how we're doing. I wouldn't have blamed you, considering what's happened, if you never again came within twenty feet of us or this home."

"Well, my uncle does live across the street. It'd be kinda hard to avoid you or this house completely, unless I stopped visiting him altogether."

The young woman looks as if she is about to burst into tears. He tries to distract: "You've got a nice place here—formal but with a warm feel to it, blue-and-white china, needlepoint pillows, some nice nineteenth-century watercolors, eighteenth-century prints, interesting mahogany pieces. . . ."

Annie finds herself surprised once more. "You have a good eye, Mr. Rourke." Damn, she thinks, I sound too formal—just like my mother.

"Call me Andrew." He chuckles. "Wondering how a roofer has such an eye, Ms. Clairmont?"

She wants to kick herself for being so thoughtless. "Well, I—"

He glances at the callouses on his palms. Lowering his voice, he says, "Sorry, I can get a bit defensive. I was a fine arts and economics major. Wanted to eat but hated corporate life, so an old friend of the family brought me into this business. It's honest work, and the only people I'm responsible to are the customers and me. It's an okay life."

The young woman notices that, while his long hands are cut up and rough, they're so beautifully shaped any woman would wish them for her own. "Call me Annie." She takes a moment to consider what to say next before replying, "To be honest, I'm not exactly corporate material either. You're lucky. I wish *I* had an old family friend who could show me the ropes to do something, something as useful as being a roofer."

Before Andrew can reply, the white-bearded coroner coming down the stairs shouts, "Well, well—Andy Rourke!" Both young people stand up as Douglas Neuman strips off his rubber gloves and drawls, "Have you gone MIA on us? Haven't seen you at the Lion's Club in a while. Other things occupying your time?" He glances at the two, hawk-like eyes peering over his wire-rimmed glasses.

"They must be, 'cause we don't see him much at CJ's either," claims Sergeant Jack Martin, grinning as he follows the coroner down the stairs.

"Not interested in getting a beer belly, sir, like Jack here. Besides, they can raise hell without any help from me." Shaking hands with Dr. Neuman, he promises, "I'll be there to give a hand for the silent auction."

Stocky, pug-nosed, Jack gives the doctor an exaggerated grin, pats his old school chum's back, and says, "The ladies are awful lonely without you, Andy."

Annie watches this knot of hale-fellow-well-met in fascination. For a moment, she even forgets why they are there, until a police officer heads toward the front door with a plastic bag containing the skull.

". . .What happens now?" she asks the coroner.

"Well, young lady, no doubt it's a human skull, but we'll have to establish age, sex, how long the person's been dead, and, if we can, determine whether there was any foul play."

"Does this mean I'm under investigation?" Annie wonders if she can bite into a chocolate and not offer any to these men.

"Couldn't it be some medical specimen, Dr. Neuman?" Andrew offers hopefully.

The older man's red suspenders peek from under his vest as he shoves his hand into his pants pockets. "Then it'd have markings to identify it as such, son."

The room suddenly falls silent, and the old gentleman, perhaps from having had so many conversations with the dead or having lived long enough to truly cherish the living, surmises a thing or two about the young people standing before him and adds, "It does appear to be older, but the state anthropologist will have to determine if this is more an item of historical interest than a criminal artifact."

Annie considers what he's said. Fighting to keep her composure, she asks, "How long will all this take? I mean, now I've got neighbors wondering whether my aunt or someone in my family is a murderer."

"It's not that uncommon to find remains," adds Jack. People, in his experience—those who have pointed the police to crime scenes—are sometimes driven by a guilty conscience, but that doesn't fit the girl who stood in front of his godfather this morning to announce that she'd found a skull—although, he has to admit, in a gutter on a roof is a new one for him.

"How long *will* all this take?" Andrew asks, unaware of having wedged himself between Annie and the others.

"Depends on how busy the office is." Adjusting the fedora on his forehead, the doctor promises, "We'll do our best. . . . You do realize," he continues, as if this information could be useful, "if this house wasn't a Victorian with gutters that wide—" the coroner holds his hands apart about a foot— "the skull would never have fit."

After the two men depart, Annie collapses onto the sofa and waves the roofer to the blue wingback opposite her.

Alma interrupts with one or two meows in order to protest the fuss. Having reconnoitered the entire room for signs of any remaining offensive behavior, she waddles up to Andrew, primly sits at his feet with all four paws neatly collected into a minute square, and introduces herself with another meow prior to making an about-face, jumping onto Annie's lap, and circling it several times to find just the right spot to sink into. The cat commences purring, a sound more like an old car engine rumbling than anything catlike. "Alma abhors anything short of quiet contentment." Annie smiles wanly as she strokes the cat.

Suddenly she becomes aware of noises from the kitchen. At that moment, Ismene marches in, navigating the tray onto the coffee table before Andrew can jump up to offer help. The tray glitters with golds, black, reds, and silver, for Ismene has pulled out the good china. A pile of tea sandwiches is heaped on one plate, and scones, still slightly warm to the touch, sit on an Imari dish next to two squat crystal bowls, one filled with fresh whipped cream and the other with raspberry jam, sterling silver spoons, forks, a teapot, and crisply starched linen. Unable to move from fatigue, Annie watches her mother quickly dispense with the pouring and serving.

As the girl inhales the strong scent of lapsang, she puzzles, "When's the last time you used the Imari, Mom?"

"When's the last time you entertained anyone of the male persuasion?" Ismene shoots back.

To break the ensuing silence, Andrew asks her about the two wild rose botanicals flanking the window.

Annie doesn't know whether to be amused or angry, particularly since her acquaintance with the young man is not even two hours old. Glancing at him—the tips of his ears have turned beet red— she wonders whether her mother perhaps has designs on him for herself. Long ago Annie accepted that Ismene will do or say exactly what she wants to and let the chips fall where they may—a characteristic one can admire from a distance, but deadly for an only child to have endured.

She pokes her pinky into the dollop of whipped cream beside

her plated scone and offers it to Alma. The cat sniffs, then laps the finger clean. Not really thinking it through, Annie exclaims, "I'm not just going to sit around and wait!"

CHAPTER 3

JOEY SAMARTINO SCANS THE AUDIENCE milling around the meeting room, which has recently been redone in textured beige wallpaper, repainted white wainscoting, café-au-lait industrial carpeting, somewhat comfortable brown-upholstered stacking chairs, and updated fluorescent lighting with brass trim. He finds that, in addition to the regular assembly of gadflies, crazies, and codgers, there are a number of less familiar faces filing in. Placing a hand on his mike to make sure no one beyond the dais can hear him, he murmurs, "Lot of energy coming from this crowd."

"Yeah, energy. Just what I need," groans Chick Accardi as he rests his clasped hands on his round belly, rocking on the back legs of his chair. "I got to get up at five tomorrow to make a sales meeting in Pennsylvania, and it looks like we're getting ready for a barbeque here with us as the main event."

"Five lousy acres," adds Eddie Polansky, yanking on his tie as if he is being choked. "We're going to be lectured on quality of life for hours—as if doing this thankless job isn't all about considering quality of life." All in all, he'd rather execute his civic duties doing what he loves best—coaching baseball, basketball, and soccer—which has led to his semi-permanent tan. But Joey long ago convinced him to come on board, and somehow, though he always means to, he's never left the council, probably out of sheer inertia and, of course, to make sure the kids aren't forgotten in the give-and-take of budget wars fought every year.

To the right of the mayor, John Kelly, freshly shaven and with the scent of Old Spice following him, tucks into his seat. Lowering his reading glasses to the tip of his nose so he can look over the rim, he assesses the audience before him and also lays his hand over his mike before whispering, "I've done some checking into what consultants would cost to tell us what we should be deciding for ourselves—a couple of thousand, about what we want to spend to renovate Northbrook Park."

"Why bother?" the mayor grumbles. "I can tell all the experts are here tonight." He can virtually predict what each of the regulars will say for and against building an office park on the parcel. It's always about feelings: Some residents don't want industry, even a clean one, to muck up their fantasies of the Mayberry they imagine they live in. Others insinuate that increased zoning density is a multi-headed monster that only lines the pockets of greedy developers and corrupt politicians. Perhaps Janet is right; his wife rarely isn't—much to his annoyance. When it becomes a burden rather than work that's enjoyable, maybe it's time to leave. Maybe he's been doing this for too long. With a barely audible exhalation, he picks up the gavel, bangs twice, and announces, "The Mayor and Council meeting will now come to order."

The regular agenda goes by fairly quickly: ordinances introduced or passed—to pay bills, post bonds, and hire people. The meeting is opened to the public. A young man with a Kennedy-style haircut and a navy-blue Armani suit strolls up to the microphone. "Robert T. Greene, 275 Pine Street," he begins. "I understand that the old DeVries property is being considered for two large office buildings?"

"Yes," the mayor replies. "The owner of the property will be submitting plans to the Planning Board shortly."

"But won't this increase traffic in an already overcrowded area?" The young man can barely refrain from turning to bask in the rising rumble of approval measured out in mummers and nods coming from the perpetually disgruntled.

"Mr. Greene—" Joey fights a tightening in his jaws, recognizing the bloodlust in Robert Greene's eyes that underscores the casual Errol Flynn pose, marking him as an unseasoned campaigner who hasn't gotten his nose bloodied by an issue or two when every politician, eventually, is stunned to discover the vagaries of public opinion. Trying not to betray his contempt, Joey slows the tempo of his voice down to a gunslinger's and continues, "Mr. Greene, we're located three miles from New York City as the crow flies. There are very few main streets in this area that don't experience rush-hour congestion. It's just the nature of the animal in this neck of the woods."

Greene sniffs. "Well, that's exactly my point. It's the woods that we're *talking* about, Mayor. An old home is being torn down, and its surrounding property, which has been literally a breath of fresh air and respite of green space albeit not open to the public, is now threatened with yet more development."

"More development?" Joey grins. "I don't understand—are you talking about the twenty townhouses that were built last year, under the Master Plan put forth not more than seven years ago? Or are you alluding to the additional ten moderate-income housing units that went up this year, and that we are required by law to provide?" Let the little bastard worm his way out of that without offense, the mayor thinks. Whatever he says will alienate someone. "What the board is considering will replace a derelict house that has been a constant eyesore and source of complaint for years while the will was contested. It has now, finally, been settled in court."

Flushing violently, then glancing at the bored reporter from the local paper sitting in the second row and about ready to flip her notebook shut, Greene counters, "Tell me, Mayor, has any progress been made by our police department on the murder discovered several days ago?"

Mystified, Samartino looks to the Borough Clerk for help. "What murder?"

Unperturbed, John replies, "There have been no reports of murders in this town. Do you mean the skull recently found on a roof of a residence in town?"

Knowing very well that the mayor was completely aware, Greene takes his best shot. "Oh, maybe you were too busy at work, mmm, selling homeowners' insurance and such, to have had the time to be made aware of—"

"This is solely in the purview of the prosecutor's office, not the local police department," Joey replies, having quickly recovered. "We haven't yet received the state pathologist's report to even determine how long the person's been dead. As you well know, Mr. Greene, as an attorney, if the skull proves to be what they consider 'historical,' the county, which oversees the investigation, may deem it unnecessary to pursue the matter further."

Greene, displaying some unexpected and irritating savvy of his own, asks, "Regardless of what the county deems appropriate, is our police department so overworked, are our streets so crime-ridden, that we can't afford the manpower to put someone to rest? It's the decent thing to do—is it not?"

At that moment, Joey decides that, after the meeting, he will seek out and ask Robert Greene to join the Planning Board and fill a seat that is soon to be vacated. The mayor has always been a great believer of the old adage "Keep your friends close and your enemies closer."

ISMENE IS STARING AT THE CROWDED WALL in the dining room filled with Aunt Ginny's artwork, which her daughter is adamant about not changing for the time being. Surely there's something that could be removed in order to incorporate the still life Ismene herself owns in some perfect way, so as to elicit little or no resistance from her daughter?

Bursting into the room, Margie gasps, "Did you *see* it?" as she dumps her blazer and bag on back of one of the lyre chairs. The young woman offers her aunt the newspaper, but Ismene, who is still considering the artwork above the credenza, remains unruffled and murmurs, "Margie, stop shouting. You're giving me a headache."

"I can't *believe* you haven't *seen* it! I mean—*everyone's* talking about it. They were asking me *tons* of questions at work today—so interested that I know all about the house and the fam—" She stops talking when she catches Ismene's frown, clears her throat, tucks an escaped lock of brown hair behind her ear, and casually asks, "Where's Annie?"

"She's been in the attic all day." Ismene grabs the paper out of her niece's hands and reads the headline. "...Anne! *Anne Elizabeth Clairmont*, come down here *now!*"

They hear a muffled "I'm busy." Realizing too late the trouble her indiscretion is about to cause, Margie leaves her aunt fuming as she continues to read the article and runs up the two flights to warn her cousin. She reaches the attic to find her on the floor, looking through stacks of yellowed papers.

"I know already," Annie offers without looking up. "Front page of the local section, under the fold. Saw it this morning when I ran some errands in town. Just didn't feel the need to share the information with Mom. So I've been up here hiding, looking for anything that could possibly shed some light on this mess." Leaning against the wall to stretch out her legs, she stares glassy-eyed at the piles of paper surrounding her.

Margie drags some boxes aside to make room to sit down, kicking up enough dust to make itself seen as well as felt. The two face each other under the harsh light from a bare bulb directly above them.

Annie continues, "It's occurred to me, much to my chagrin, that maybe I really didn't know Aunt Ginny as well as I thought. I mean, maybe there's more to her that we don't know."

"Like she murdered someone?"

"*No!*" Annie snaps. "...Well, maybe. I don't know what to think at this point." She rubs her eyes hard; the dust is finally getting to her. "Dammit, I saw a fairly serene woman. But did my expectations demand that of her as an antidote to my mother? Did I miss who she was because of my own selfishness?"

"Ah." Margie rolls her eyes. "It would be *just* like you to take the blame for something that doesn't remotely involve you at all." But she feels guilty about getting her cousin in trouble, and murmurs, "Sorry, I had no idea Auntie didn't know."

Annie shrugs off the instantaneous realization that dinner will be a crescendo of I-told-you-sos, pulls out a photo album, and offers it her cousin. "If you want to help, take a look at this. It's all pretty routine—I've seen a lot of these before—except for this picture here. Do you know these people?" She points to a black-and-white photo of Aunt Ginny in the backyard with a young man and woman, all waving at the camera.

"...No one I know. They certainly don't look like family." Margie holds up the photo underneath the light for a closer look; without looking up, she asks, "Let me take this home and ask my mother if she knows who they are."

"Okay, but don't lose it. For now, though, take that pile of papers over there and look for anything that could possibly explain why a skull ended up on Aunt Ginny's roof. And since you tipped off my mother that the family has made the paper for something other than the announcement of a birth, marriage, or death, please stay for dinner and run interference for me."

Before Margie can beg off, they hear Ismene's footsteps on the stairs. Flinging the attic door open, military-erect and nostrils flaring, she barks, "Even as a child you had your father's ridiculous need to tell the truth, as if all the sentimental tripe about honesty really means a damn thing in this world, where people are...*weak!*" She practically spits out the disagreeable word.

No one moves. She continues, "Of course the truth can set you free, saddling the one you've unburdened yourself to with the weight of your confession! Lying, on the other hand, is a cross *everyone* bears—not only the one who carries the lie, but also the person lied to." Ismene takes a breath, willing herself not to even *think* about crying. "*No one* gets off scot-free, no matter what is done in the name of truth. Have I made myself perfectly clear?"

CHAPTER 4

NDREW SWINGS OPEN THE DOOR to his drinking haunt of choice, CJ's, just outside the town limits: easy enough to slip discreetly through the safety of local streets, and not as likely to have everyone in town breathing down your neck. The blond wood paneling and low wattage of the brass sconces keep the clientele forever good-looking, and the grizzle-haired bartender with the knife scar across his chin is glancing at the clock, then the customers, to see whether it's about the right time to lower the lights further. He asks out of politeness, "The usual?" before pouring Andrew a beer.

Jack Martin, off-duty, comes barreling through the door and acknowledges the roofer's presence with a slap on the back. "How you doin', pal?"

"Been better, been worse." Taking a long swallow, Andrew inquires, "How's Rachel?"

The cop's right shoulder rolls forward, marking territory. "They tell me it's part of the routine. She's got me paintin' this and fixin' that—drivin' me nuts." He takes another sip of beer. Shrugging off his mystification, he continues, "But it's supposed to be normal—this nesting activity."

Andrew breaks into a grin. "...You old dog, no! A father. Oh, God, now I've heard everything. Congratulations."

They dig a good-natured punch into each other's shoulder. After a bit of small talk about baby showers and due dates, Jack eventually gets down to business, and Andrew listens bemused as his childhood friend pulls rank as expectant father to point a finger at him and advise, "You know what I'm saying—at thirty, you're not getting any younger."

"Yeah, yeah."

They drink in silence for a while. Jack finally breaks it to confess, "What's with this monk routine? The girls used to flock to you, kid. I admit I was a bit jealous of all that attention you got until I lucked out with Rachel. You know how it is with cops and divorce. But she wanted me anyway—even my crazy family. How good is that?"

"The flock didn't want *me*," growls Andrew, staring at his nearly empty glass. "They wanted my earning potential, working for that investment bank. Women talk big about not wanting to be treated like an object. The truth was, they turned *me* into just *that*. I could practically see dollar signs in their eyes."

To prevent him from getting too glum, Jack says, "What about that skinny one with the curly hair—Anne, uh, Anne Clairmont? Nice-looking, presentable, seems to have a mind of her own and enough money not to care *what* you do." Jack can't keep from chuckling when he adds, "Eh, a little nervous, though, maybe a murderer—but, hey, no one's perfect."

"It's Annie, actually. And mind of her own is an understatement. She's a prickly one, and her mother is a handful, too. . . . Have you gotten back the forensic report from the anthropology lab?" Andrew asks casually, shifting the conversation to more neutral ground.

"Not yet, it's only been a week. But," Jack drawls, "don't expect anything very soon. All this scientific investigation takes time."

A couple of patrons shout their hellos as Joey Samartino, and two councilmen who are most closely associated with him, appear. The mayor spots the young men, whom he hasn't touched base with for a while, and makes it a point to shake their hands and exchange pleasantries about baseball and which team will make the upcoming playoffs.

As they move to one of the well-polished wooden tables across from the bar, the mayor eyes Andrew in mock seriousness. "So I have you to thank for my latest headache." Placing his lit cigar carefully on the rim of the ashtray, he jokes, "Why couldn't you find long-lost treasure up on that roof instead, and then convince that waif to fund my campaign?"

"Good! You're running?" Jack exclaims before he can think better of it, but he has been hating even the slightest possibility of having to report to Greene as mayor. Two years ahead of him in school, and even then Greene was all about brown-nosing teachers. Jack's sure that Greene hasn't forgotten how easy it was for him to break the bastard's nose after he tried to manhandle Mary at a party. His sister came home crying but hadn't wanted to make a fuss; Jack had decided to even the score *his* way. It was worth being kicked out of school for a week; neither he nor Greene had admitted to school authorities why the fight started. At least the little prick had that shred of decency in him.

"After my opponent's performance the other night, do I really have an option? I don't mind being voted out of office—that's the people's choice—but damned if I don't run again, and they think it's because I'm scared."

Chick Accardi starts singing, "'Do not forsake me, o, my darlin','" and the men crack up picturing the mayor and Greene in a face-off down the center of Main Street.

"Yeah, well, it's not going to be so pretty next year. This kid's out for blood. Wants to make his spurs on the back of *'old-time'* politics," grumbles Eddie Polansky, wiping his glasses clean and adjusting them behind his rather elephantine ears.

"*I'd* say all bets are off," Chick agrees, fingering his pack of cigarettes, sighing, and placing them back in his jacket without lighting up. "Question is. . .what are we going to do about it?"

Silence settles in for a second or two as each of them considers the possibilities.

ACROSS TOWN ON WALNUT STREET, MRS. CHRISTINA HILL, one of those extraordinary women who is doing just fine at age eighty-eight, grabs the madeira bottle. Molded by the Depression, jazz, and the loss of her husband twenty-one years ago, she finds reading and music far more satisfying than just about anything else. These days, nothing pleases her more than to see nice families moving into the old neighborhood. Maybe, as the twentieth century draws to a close with all its predicted apocalyptic eventualities—with each new family arrival, there's a chance they'll bring up the young right, slowing things down to a more human pace, even if for a brief moment—

and, what the hell, a moment is all Christina Hill is asking for.

Remembering how Annie blossomed into a noisier, happier child under Ginny's tutelage when she visited her aunt three houses down the block, the old woman is delighted that Annie is now her neighbor and sitting with her as she pours madeira into two green cut-crystal glasses. She knocks hers back and sighs. Her smile shifts the fine wrinkles that ripple over her white skin, her apple-shaped cheeks rouged to compete with the flaming red of her lacquered nails. "Your Aunt Ginny was okay. A real lady who never was stuck up about anybody or anything."

Annie's face clouds over; she picks up her own glass and takes a swallow, hoping to shoo away the blues. She grabs some chocolate-covered coffee beans out of a covered cabbage-rose candy dish that, as a child, she used to raid during her visits to Mrs. Hill's—where in the summer they watched soap operas and drank ice cream sodas concocted from 7-Up and Breyer's vanilla—and pops one into her mouth. Mrs. Hill's living room has remained absolutely the same since those childhood visits: hunter green walls and leopard-skin throw pillows on white chairs and sofa, the ultimate in Fifties *luxe* and completely incompatible with the well-used candy dish and old-fashioned crystal on the ornately carved and marble-topped coffee table.

The former chorus girl, who's seen just about everything at least twice, pretends not to notice Annie's roller coaster emotional ride. "It always seemed to me that it didn't matter whether a body was a grocer or in charge of some big company, Ginny sailed through, chatting people up as if, well, as if nothing mattered more than *that* person, right then and there. She hit the mark, whether they needed a good laugh or a sympathetic ear."

Fingering her empty glass, Mrs. Hill muses for the hundredth time about her lifelong neighbor. "Must have suffered a great deal in order to be able to do it as well as she did."

Annie sits up in alarm. "Why do you say that?" What if the skull *has*, after all, something to do with her great-aunt, and she's stupidly exposed the one person she's always loved best? Maybe her mother is right. What a thought.

Reaching over to turn on a lamp—the smell of a wood fire burning somewhere in the neighborhood drifts through the open window as dusk disappears, darkening the room—Mrs. Hill continues, "In life, we all get some kind of blow to the stomach that's hard to recover from."

"Like losing her fiancé?"

"Maybe. A heart's tricky to judge, my dear. No one is an open book. Never forget that!" Leaning forward in her chair, Christina confides, "People have to choose how to *deal* with the world after a disaster—*that* shows what you're made of. They either become cynical, wanting their half in the middle. Or nervous, spending the rest of their lives waiting for the next blow and, most of the time, successfully arranging it. But precious few ever learn to be more patient with people's follies."

"...Where does the skull come in?"

Mrs. Hill shrugs. "Who the hell knows? Have you gone through her letters yet? Ginny wrote tons of letters. She must have gotten a few in return."

"Over the years I got two bundles from her myself. Considered myself lucky to." Discouraged, Annie kicks her legs out in front of her and stretches them briefly before continuing, "Been up to the attic, but it's so packed that I've made barely a dent there. There are bank records going back decades, receipts filed by year, keepsake clothing—including a couple of her hats I found in a stack of hat boxes that are so cool I might start wearing them." She pops another chocolate coffee bean in her mouth and considers what to say next. "But so far, nothing to show why a skull ended up on her roof."

The doorbell rings, disrupting the coziness that has settled over the room. Both women answer it to find a sincere-looking young man facing them.

"Hello, ladies. My name is Robert Greene. I'm planning to run for mayor next year. I'd like to talk to you about getting your support." As soon as Mrs. Hill notices Annie reaching to straighten her hair, she asks the well-dressed young man to come in. While he is facing her out of respect, his bedroom eyes have zeroed in on Annie. "It's time for a change in town politics—a fresh outlook on old problems. Can't do that with the same old faces year in and year out."

Giggling, Christina offers, "Well, young man, I've had my face for over eighty years, and I'm very content with the routine of waking up and seeing it every morning."

Annie laughs, so Robert follows suit, somewhat confused. To cover it up, he remarks, "Well, there's no substitute for wisdom," before returning to his point. "But the good ol' boy smoky back rooms are just not conducive to *good* politics these days. . . ."

Annie's mind wanders back to four days ago, when the mayor offered a chair and some coffee in an effort to appease her mother after the initial shock of her revelation. She remembers him, and particularly the borough clerk John Kelly, being very considerate.

"...And the overzealous building that's taken place in this town is disgraceful! I joined the Planning Board recently to put a stop to it before it's too late to act on other options."

The doorbell rings again, and Mrs. Hill says hello to Andrew, standing awkwardly in front of her. He returns her greeting and is asked to come in. About to hail Annie, he's startled to see her talking to another guy.

"What are *you* doing here?" she squeaks when she looks up to find Andrew before her.

Acutely aware of wearing his work-weary black tee shirt, jeans, and scuffed black boots, he offers, "Um, your mother." He tries to smooth the tee, hoping the two beers aren't apparent in his behavior or on his breath. "I went to your house with some information, and your mother said you were here and to come by."

"My mother!" Annie's frown is fierce enough to make him move back involuntarily.

Two additional glasses appear on the coffee table. Hardly able to contain her mirth, Mrs. Hill inquires, "Well, Andrew, how's your mother doing? I haven't seen Muriel for quite a while. I think it was a year ago, at the funeral home for Herb Tyler's wake. May he rest in peace. Have some madeira. You, too, Robert. I think everyone could use a bit right now."

The doorbell rings yet again. Glumly, Annie grumbles, "Let me guess," and Ismene glides into the room and through introductions to the young politician as well as another friendly hello to the roofer, whom she almost forcibly pushes onto one of the chairs before he can escape out the door. She kisses Christina a warmish hello before settling down in the best seat, next to the old woman, ramrod erect.

She crosses her legs, folds both hands on her knee, smiles sweetly, and asks, "Well, whatever am I missing?"

Thrilled to have doubled his audience in a matter of minutes, Robert clears his throat. "We've been talking about the overbuilding taking place in town. Seems no one has really given much fore-thought to the long-term impact. We need to revisit the town's master plan before it's too late. There just aren't enough open spaces around for people to enjoy."

"We've got four parks in a town that's only three-point-nine miles square," growls Andrew, who has finally placed Greene as one of the upperclassman in high school that nobody liked.

"Well, as a lawyer involved in the business world from day to day ...."

Andrew glowers at his arrogance. Ismene, who is always appalled by *other* people's bad behavior, gives Robert a once-over. "How in-teresting you're a lawyer. My father studied law, too. Never practiced it, though. He considered it too plebeian." And without waiting for the reply that won't come, she continues, "Tell me, young man, do you wear baseball caps?"

Annie demands, "What is *wrong* with more parks?"

"Why, yes." Nonplussed by Ismene's question and eager to further his agenda, Robert proudly tells her, "I have quite a collection of them."

"*You* don't strike me as the type that wears those silly caps, An-drew. *Do* you?" Ismene purrs.

"Only to play ball, ma'am," Andrew answers as he tries to follow this strange woman's thinking and ventures to add, "I'd rather wear my halfsies—my helmet, that is—to ride my motorcycle."

A rather guttural murmur escapes Ismene's lips, gone slack as she muses over this last piece of rather appealing information. She sips madeira that has appeared before her, refusing to acknowledge Annie, who is apoplectic at being ignored by just about everyone and repeating her question about parks.

"I must admit," interrupts Mrs. Hill, "I've always thought Joey's done a good job of running this town. Taxes been steady for the last three years, and when you're on a fixed income, that's a blessing."

"When you're a homeowner—" Andrew is now addressing Annie's question— "you've got to think about taxes, too. Would you risk the town being forced to choose between a hike in taxes or cuts in services, which realistically means either borough employees don't get raises or—worse—lose their jobs, for another *park?*"

"There *are* other options," Robert diplomatically offers without naming them.

"Are you saying I'm not realistic?" Annie snaps at Andrew.

"No, I'm *saying*, give the situation some thought before chasing a pretty picture wrapped up in a bow."

"Really, Annie," Ismene chides, "becoming sanctimonious even about grass and trees, is simply not *attractive*."

In an attempt to regain control of the situation, Robert says, "Besides, there are other issues to consider."

Andrew barely hesitates at this opportunity to show Robert Greene for the prick he is. Giving him a sidelong glance, he innocently repeats, "Other issues?"

"Well, the town seems to be dragging its heels with this latest event. I mean, nothing has been done about that skull."

No one moves, and the silence builds. Andrew, wanting to kick himself for behaving like a jerk at Annie's expense, says, "Annie, I'm—"

The young woman, furious, jumps up and takes deliberate strides toward him, who meets her half way.

"You're *despicable*," she barks. "Scoring debating points at *my* expense." Giving her best effort to be Ismene-like, she levels at him her deadliest insult: "You, sir, are no gentleman!" and before anyone can respond, the front door slams shut.

"Well, now," Ismene muses before taking another sip of her drink, "she *has* taken notice of the young man."

CHAPTER 5

I SMENE LONG AGO DECIDED the young take themselves far too seriously—her daughter, in particular, overdoes the need to be a good girl—and, maternal loyalties aside, she finds this behavior on the whole tedious. Not that it is such a bad thing when it comes to her own immediate needs; one can always get somewhere by exercising a measured bit of arm-twisting with Annie. However, Ismene still hopes that the girl will eventually learn from her example.

She sighs to no one as she dumps the remains of Mr. Handelman's blown roses into the kitchen trash. Sincerity is so boring without some grit! Even the simplest of lives can be lived with a modicum of adventure. The humdrum creeps in fast enough if a person doesn't keep vigil.

That capacity to live is what she had liked best about Aunt Ginny. While the woman was a *paragon* of consideration, there was nothing sentimental about her and no apologies made for being single in a culture that remains less than forgiving to unattached women.

Squeezing the dishcloth dry and folding it into place, she stares out the kitchen window to observe a squirrel and a robin going about their business around the ample yard, completely indifferent to each other's existence. Behind them a red fox crosses the yard, along with her kits, and disappears behind a holly bush. Life goes by so quickly. Ismene sighs and immediately puts *that* thought out of her head. She instead becomes uncomfortably aware of another question rising in her heart—why did Aunt Ginny love *Annie* best?

Alma chooses this moment to jump onto a ladder-back chair nearest Ismene at the kitchen table and do her ritual circular dance before finally lying down to announce her satisfaction with the world through her rumble of a purr. The ordeal of the unexpected has ceased—no more hospice nurses, moving boxes, policemen, or extraneous family traipsing in and out of her space, for Alma lived quietly with Ginny, a gifted caregiver.

Scratching her behind one ear, Ismene looks down affectionately. "I promise you a more civilized life than you've had for the last couple of months, but you don't mind if I also try to move things along in the hopes of having grandchildren one day—do you?" Alma gives her a mournful look, jumps off the chair, and departs for the dining room, leaving Ismene to wonder how in the world her daughter can elicit such loyalty, even from animals. It's beyond her comprehension.

She decides to try to make peace with the cat; it's bad enough that Annie isn't speaking to her, as if yesterday evening's debacle was *her* fault instead of that silly twit's who's running for mayor. She follows Alma up the stairs and into the study where, instead of heading for the bargello pillow thrown against the arm of the couch—her accustomed napping spot—the cat leaps effortlessly off the sofa back but misses the bookshelf and lands on the oak end table. A vase filled with hydrangea from the garden tumbles off, and Alma, to hide her embarrassment and pass off the gaff as intentional, paws at a carved wooden box on the bookshelf, sending it crashing to the floor, too. Several keys clatter about. Alma, having preserved her dignity, hops back onto the couch and settles down to nap against her pillow, pretending she has done nothing out of the ordinary.

Ismene grabs some paper toweling from a linen closet in the hallway filled with cleaning supplies. As she sorts through the mess, having pushed aside the oak end table, she finds—to her amazement—no water on the pine floor, as if the accident didn't happen at all. With a shrug, she replaces the box and keys on the shelf as well as the now-chipped white vase refilled with water and flowers on the end table.

But before she pushes the end table into place, something about the vanished water nags at her. She takes a look at the floorboards and starts tapping on them with a knuckle until she works out where one sounds hollow. Grabbing a pen knife from the desk drawer, she eventually pries up the board and finds a locked metal box damp with water, but no key. She smiles, reaches for the box that Alma fortuitously knocked off the shelf, and tries every one of the keys till she finds the one that fits.

The box is filled with letters tied with a blue ribbon. As she looks through them, it becomes clear they are all to and from the same person. Ismene decides that Annie isn't the only one capable of sleuthing and settles onto the couch to find out why these letters needed to be hidden.

THE LITTLE SHOP IS EXACTLY THAT, a sliver of space in one of the smallest of commercial storefronts on Main Street, which manages to survive by selling high-quality hot beverages, loose coffee and tea, chocolates, homemade cookies, and slices of cake. If you want a cold beverage, except in the middle of summer when the owner, Rob Bradley, may make a batch of iced Earl Grey, he suggests you go down the block to Dunkin' Donuts to get your fix. He's not in the least bit interested in selling anything that panders to the uninitiated. The black-and-white checkerboard linoleum floor and white beadboard walls of the shop haven't been updated, which suits the owner just fine. This work is his labor of love. And since he owns the building, his shop, his rules.

The bell tinkles. Annie walks in, mulling whether to buy some Darjeeling or oolong as a peace offering to her mother. She sees Mrs. Hill and Mr. Handelman conversing at the counter. Before she can consider whether she can slip out unnoticed, Mr. Handelman hails her to join them in a cup of coffee. In the meantime, Mrs. Hill places her order. "Could I have a pound and a half of chocolate-dipped orange peel?" she brightly asks.

"Dark chocolate?" Bradley replies though he already knows the answer.

"Oh, dark, of course. And the chocolate coffee beans, too—another pound."

"Mrs. Hill," Annie blurts out, "I'm *so* sorry for the way I behaved last night. It's just, well, Andrew Rourke makes me furious."

Christina manages to nod gravely. "You don't say."

Rudy, alarmed, asks, "What in heaven's name did my nephew do to upset you, dear girl?"

Annie thrusts out her chin. "He's just *such* a know-it-all! As if he's the only political expert in this town. He simply didn't want to hear anything that Robert Greene had to say about parks."

"Ah!" He adds some milk and sugar to his cup, stirring thoughtfully before continuing, "My nephew is a bit protective when it comes to the mayor. He was Andrew's baseball coach for many years. As a youth—only for a short time, you understand—my nephew had a wild streak, and there was no talking to him. He and his best friend Jack would get up to all sorts of mischief. But the mayor took him in hand and taught him to plough that energy into baseball and civic responsibility. Andrew remains loyal to those who have been good to him."

"Mmmh, good chocolate," says Christina, as she offers some chocolate orange peel to Annie and Mr. Handelman. "Too bad you feel that way, Annie. Always thought he was an interesting one, that Andy."

"Interesting?"

"There's a brooding side to him."

"Brooding?"

"You know, Heathcliff-brooding. Mind you, he's always been a smart young man, good at sports, popular with the girls for sure. And well-regarded for the charity work he does. But there's a side to him that remains very, very private."

Annie sniffs, "Well, he told me about how he gave up banking. . .but he forgot to mention being a ladies' man."

No longer able to keep a straight face as she pays for the chocolates, Christina giggles, fire-engine red lips forming a perfect circle. "No, I suppose he was saving that for later. Guess he also hasn't told you what his real love is yet."

Before Annie can pretend she isn't interested in finding out, John Kelly calls out, "I *thought* it was you," as he sails through the door. "Hello, young lady. How's tricks?" He kisses Christina's over-rouged cheek, shakes Rudy Handelman's hand, asking whether his gardening business was affected by the recent rains, then turns to Annie to inquire, "How are you holding up?" He pours himself a cup of tea from the daily-special canister, stirs in two sugars and takes a sip. "Wow, it smells like smoke. What is it?"

"Lapsang souchong," replies Annie absent-mindedly. "One of my favorites."

"Kind of fancy for me, having grown up Lipton, but I'll indulge myself a bit. Rob, could I have a quarter of a pound of that tea, and a pound of French Roast, automatic drip?"

Christina holds out her bag of orange-peel chocolates and indicates he should help himself. She shouts over the noise of the grinder to make herself heard, "Been reading the paper. I see Joey has competition this year."

"Competition is good. That's my mantra." John raps his knuckles on the wooden counter for emphasis. "Keeps this country strong, you know." He mumbles something about a diet before grabbing a piece or two of chocolate and bends toward Christina to make sure he doesn't miss a word she says.

"A very nice young man came knocking on my door last night to tell me we don't have enough open space in town."

"Interesting." John bites into the orange peel, wrinkling his nose before taking another swallow of tea.

"Well, you know how I feel about Joey." She takes another piece of chocolate before tucking both bags into her oversized navy purse. "But that bright young thing is all get-up-and-go about bringing in *good* government."

Shrugging off his annoyance, John replies, "Look, Greene's ambitious enough, and he'll probably go far. I'm just sorry to see such a contentious campaign *within* the party where issues are muddled up with swipes at personalities."

A silence prevails as the grinder finishes up the order, which Annie breaks. "I'm afraid, Mr. Kelly, that my family and the skull have become part of the campaign, too."

"Call me John. I know." He grabs his order and pays for it. "I'm sorry it's so awkward for you. . . . If I get the connection right, you're a relative of Ginny Spencer, right?"

Annie nods. "My great-aunt."

"Just about everybody in town was her student, and I've never heard an unkind word about her. Tell me, was there any bad blood between the Greenes and your aunt?"

"No," answers Rudy on Annie's behalf. "I saw students come in and out of her home for tutoring all the time. Miss Ginny went out of her way to help those who needed it most—especially students who couldn't afford to pay for tutoring, or who had some other kind of special circumstance. Her goodness was like a shield of protection. Most of the children in town took advantage of the Mischief Night to wrap rolls of tissue paper around their teachers' front yards, but never hers."

Kelly, as he mulls over this information, takes another appreciative sip of his tea. "Well, with any luck, the good people will remember that the mayor's done right by them. The town's clean and safe, taxes are steady, and folks on both sides of the aisle get help with their problems. But the voting public is a fickle lot, and this incident is far more entertaining than drawn-out discussions about budgets."

"Or parks," Annie sighs.

CHAPTER 6

PAUL DEMARIA PRACTICALLY LEAPS off his kitchen steps, barely missing the holly bush at the edge of his property as he runs to catch up with the mayor, panting, "Hey, Joey—"

"Paul!" The mayor waves the butt end of his cigar, squinting against the bright light, and grins. "Fancy meeting you here."

Pulling his tan windbreaker a tad closer against the chilly breeze, Paul mumbles, "Gee, Joey, what a creepy thing to find at the Spencer house, a skull!"

The mayor blows a cloud of smoke upward and inquires, "What do *you* make of this predicament, and our esteemed junior high school principal?"

"Ginny Spencer a murderer? Can't imagine it."

"Frankly, neither can I. In fact, I have rather fond memories, while in school, of admiring her legs. However tough she was as an administrator, she did have great legs."

Paul respectfully pauses to consider this before spilling out in one huge breath, "If you ask me, she was a bit on the skinny side. I really had a hard time, if you know what I mean, keeping my mind on social studies when Miss Graziano stood in front of the class." Blushing (he suddenly remembers his wife and daughter lecturing him about being a chauvinist), he stammers in his defense, "I mean, one *can*, without saying a word, still admire a womanly figure, from a. . .a respectful distance, even these days, no?"

"Oh, I believe so, Paul," says Samartino, cigar safely tucked back into his mouth. Catching a whiff of honeysuckle mingled with tobacco as they walk toward the borough hall, the mayor again looks up at the clouds sailing by at a clip. They seemed to him a lot like the promises of youth, drifting along until suddenly they are out of sight.

"Wonder why she never married? She was good looking, made nice money, had enough male companionship to be sure, and she could certainly hold her liquor when occasion called for it—nothing prissy about her, definitely a plus. Yet always the lady."

"Hilda was just telling me at breakfast that she remembers her friend Carol Schetino—you know, the Schetinos that live on the other end of town—who heard from *her* girlfriend that, once, at one of those wedding shower things, Ginny Spencer was asked why she wasn't married. She said she'd been in love two times in her life, and that was more than enough for her heart to take."

"Maybe it's a jilted lover up in that gutter!" Joey knocks the ashes from his cigar.

"You mean a woman scorned? Naw, she never seemed the flighty type."

Samartino grunts in agreement.

". . .I hate tellin' tales, Joey, but they say you're not moving on this case because you're afraid to ruffle people's feathers and lose votes. Bottom line, they're saying you're runnin' scared this election."

"Yeah, I've heard the same garbage, too." The mayor once more looks up, admiring the lightness of the clouds drifting by.

Paul watches him stare at nothing for a moment or two. "The Greene family's always showing off," Paul cautiously says. "Puttin' on airs, like they're better than everyone else. And boy, what that Harriet Greene thinks of her darling son Robert, and *don't she tell everyone!*"

"Yeah?"

Puzzled at his indifference, Paul asks, "Aren't you mad, Joey? You don't sound mad."

With a sigh, Joey shifts his gaze back to Earth. "Thing is, Paulie—don't get mad, get even. Anyway, showboating as the perfect family is always a tip-off for me. You don't have to look hard to find some chink in that shiny armor everyone sees." With a curse, he relights his cigar and exhales. What a pain in the ass this is—yet it never hurts to learn all you can about your opponent. "Paul, I need your help. Isn't Harriet Greene part of the Ahearn clan? Weren't there something like seven or eight brothers and sisters in that brood?"

ROBERT GREENE RETURNS THE PHONE to its cradle and begins to massage his temples, trying to fend off one of his headaches. He lowers the blinds to dim the bright morning light coming into his office. Once again, his mother has let him know exactly where he's fallen short in filial obligation—from lacking a steady girlfriend and by extension not providing her with grandchildren, to reminding him about the sacrifice she's made, a small loan, for which she charges interest, to help him furnish his office—the list gets trotted out whenever no one is around. It's always about *her* all-consuming needs.

He takes solace as he looks up from his desk to survey the Miro litho above the blond Scandinavian credenza, mid-century, in his inner office with satisfaction. It looks right. It suggests up-and-coming yet not without a sense of deep culture. Nonetheless, it has been his hard work that has built up a clientele, as well as maneuvering for the appointment to the Planning Board that will make people sit up and take notice of him, enough to recognize where the future lies. And God bless the good townsfolk, some of whom are already willing to place him at the helm, to break the Tammany Hall grip that those old codgers with their drip-dry shirts have had for far too long.

He feels better when he thinks of how sunny the future looks. Uncle Bobby has promised to introduce him to people who count. Not bad to have a sitting superior court judge throw a party where he'd naturally include his family along with his friends and colleagues. One can meet and greet some pretty important people under the most favorable of circumstances—while drinking someone else's liquor. Surely, this is only the beginning.

The secretary, Kathy Armsted, buzzes him. "Mr. Greene, Miss Lara Snow is here to see you."

"...Snow?"

"Your cousin—"

"Oh, yes. Of course. First, please come in and take these files. Then show her in." This visitor was the reason that his mother called. To remind him that he was required to show a farm girl from the

Oklahoma branch of the family around.

Knowing her boss all too well, Kathy closes the door behind her before reaching for the work. As he hands her the files, he whispers, "Well, is she country-bumpkin enough to cramp my style?"

"Actually, she'd improve your style tremendously, considering she's young, about five-seven, blonde, green-eyed, gorgeous, and you should be so lucky."

"Ah!" Greene starts straightening his dark gray tie and reaches for the charcoal pinstripe jacket hanging on the back of his chair. "Wonder if she's my second or third cousin?"

"I didn't hear that." Opening the office door, Kathy, glad her boss is not a mind-reader, murmurs, as she returns to her desk, "I'll get this to you shortly, Mr. Greene. Right this way, Miss Snow."

At the sight of Lara Snow entering his office, Greene jumps from his chair so quickly he doesn't completely clear his desk. He tries not to wince in pain as he pulls out one of the two chairs for her.

She sinks gracefully onto the seat, smiles her thanks, and folds her hands onto her lap. "So good of you to take time out of your busy schedule to see me. Aunt Harriet's told me so much about you that I feel I've known you all my life." As she flashes another smile, along with a tilt of her head, Robert notices her perfect teeth.

"What brings you here—business, pleasure, or both?"

"Mostly, to meet my grandmother's family. But I must admit, I was dying to see as much of the country as possible, so I traveled here by train. It was stunning. You should try traveling by train sometimes."

"Sounds. . .intriguing. Are you afraid to fly?"

"No, not at all. It's just that I've never had the opportunity to travel out of state. And I must confess, ever since I was a little girl, I've always longed to see big-city lights, and there's nowhere bigger or brighter than New York."

"Well, *we* certainly like to think so. . . ." Positioning himself at the edge of his chair so he's leading his advance with well-formed biceps, he asks, "Perhaps you'd like to go out for dinner tonight—to the Village, eightish?"

"You mean *Greenwich* Village? Oh, I'd *love* to. I've heard terrific things about it."

"There's a charming place I know with a quiet garden where we might be able to dine alfresco if the weather is just right. I could tell you all about my campaign."

LATER THAT AFTERNOON, ANNIE UNLOCKS the black wooden door to her home, a bag of oolong tea in hand purchased as a truce with her mother. The girl long ago learned it simply isn't worth the energy expended to be angry at Ismene for long. It accomplishes very little to attempt to hold one's own against a force of nature. More often than not, the result is she is reduced to a mere particle floating on waves of her mother's effusions for or against one thing or another.

As she enters, the smell of coffee, always a red flag re Ismene, wafts through as she drops her bag, keys, and tea on the hall table.

She finds her mother entertaining in the parlor. "Oh, do come in, Annie," drawls the latter, as if the house belongs to her. "Let me introduce my daughter, Anne Clairmont. This is Lara Snow. Apparently, her grandmother was a friend of Aunt Ginny's."

Annie's interest is piqued; she offers her hand to the stunning blonde and is somewhat surprised to receive a limp one in return, a sensation that leaves her feeling her strong handshake was somehow uncouth. "Oh, really? When did they know each other?"

"Long time ago. You see, Grandmother and I were very, very close. She told me all sorts of things, stories about growing up here in town, her brothers playing in the caves where they grew mushrooms along the Palisades, how the boys would dare each other to ride the ice floes coming from upriver in the spring, how the McMullen boy ended up being picked up by the New York Harbor Police because his was rapidly going out to sea. . . ."

Annie giggles. "Yes, I've heard those stories, too. It seems poor Tommy McMullen's fifteen minutes of fame had to do with a slab of melting ice." Still unable to shake off feeling inadequate after that handshake, she does her best to regain her composure, perched upright on the wingback and catching herself before she grabs cookies to make up for not having had lunch. Instead, she selects one chocolate chip cookie, breaks it in half, and takes a nibble. "Was your grandmother's last name Snow?"

"No, she grew up as Sylvia Ahearn."

"You've *met* members of the Ahearn family, darling," Ismene murmurs. "That young man running for office, you know, the one with the baseball hats?"

Mother and daughter don't exchange looks; they're far too well-mannered to risk making their guest uncomfortable.

To lower the temperature in the room, Annie politely inquires, "How did your grandmother and my great-aunt meet?"

"They became friends after they realized their boyfriends served together, you see. Here, I have a picture of them." Annie studies the two smiling women, one in her late teens, the other in her mid-twenties, sitting in the back yard under the oak tree laughing. There is something familiar about the young girl's face, but she can't place where she's seen it before. "Although my grandmother was a senior in high school, she was exceptional. Your great-aunt took notice and became her friend."

"Oh, oh, yes! *Now* I remember where I've seen this girl before. There's a photo of her, a man, and my aunt Ginny in the garden. I'd show it to you, but I gave it to my cousin to ask her mother if she knew who was in the photo with Aunt Ginny."

"If the young man is handsome, it must be my grandfather, Buddy."

Ismene makes no comment as she concentrates on pouring more coffee into Lara's cup. Handing the cup back, she asks the young woman how long she plans to visit.

Lara drawls, "It all depends on how long each of my aunts and uncles will allow me to stay with them. Who knows," she laughs, "maybe I'll fall in love with someone here and never go back."

At a loss for small talk, Annie is somewhat relieved when Lara says, "This is such a beautiful house. I'd love to see it, since I've heard *so* much about it. Would you mind showing me?"

"Sure, I practically grew up here. Obviously right across the hall-way is the dining room, and the kitchen is right behind it, where you can step onto the porch and into the garden. I have such lovely memories of summer picnics in the backyard under the oak tree, with lots of lemonade and gossip."

Eventually the young women drift upstairs. "The first room was my great-aunt's. No one's occupying it right now." The scent of gardenia, Ginny's perfume, still lingers in the room. For a moment Annie imagines she can hear her aunt call out her name.

Annie, however, is startled out of her reverie when her guest, without permission, enters the room to take a closer look. Lara lifts open the japanned wooden music box and listens to *"Für Elise"* for a moment, studies the needlepoint carpet with the tree-of-life motif, and touches the French blue silk moiré drapes that match the bedspread as she glances out the window. She murmurs to herself, "Not hers."

Somewhat startled by this remark, Annie is about to suggest they take a look in the garden when Lara repeats, "Not hers at all."

"Who, my aunt? But I feel her here all the time, even now." Furious at herself for her confusion and for bungling it so that this stranger seems somehow to have gotten the upper hand, Annie tries to remain civil. "Why don't I show you the flower beds out back that Aunt Ginny so prized?"

A WEEK LATER, MARGIE, SITTING ON ANNIE'S BED, takes one look at her cousin and groans. "Couldn't you for once not dress like a librarian in training?" Before Annie can answer, Margie pulls a black item out of a plastic tote bag and hands it to her. "Don't even try conning your way out of this skirt. I will not go to the hottest restaurant in town with you looking like Jane Eyre!" She sits at the edge of the bed, hands folded, adding, "Nor do I need to sit around feeling sorry for you as Auntie's little comments about how dull your outfit is spark forth all night long. We are going out to celebrate your mother's birthday—you, me, and Jim! Let's have some fun. Lord knows, with this skull business, we can all use some!"

Ignoring the skirt, Annie faces the mirror in her bedroom and takes a brown eyeliner to her lids, deepening the line already there, then smudging it with her finger. She yanks open the top drawer to her dresser, finds and applies a burgundy gloss over the taupe lipstick already in place. For good measure, she daubs the back of each ear with her aunt's perfume. Finally, she shimmies out of her navy trousers, silently thanks the gods for having had the sense to shave her legs before she dressed, throws off her oversized cotton shirt, and finally zips up the form-fitting skirt. She opens her closet and fishes out a bright red silk shirt her mother gave her for Christmas last year, which Annie considers far too revealing for her tastes—tag still in place. Slipping into black heels, she takes a look at herself in the mirror. She replaces her pearl studs with a pair of gold drop earrings finished with tiny rubies. Stepping back from the mirror, she does an about-face and steels herself for her cousin's critique.

"Oh, thank goodness! You look like you belong in this century."

Ismene knocks and pops her head in. Taking in the clothing draped all over the furniture and seeing her daughter morphed from a timid soul into a good-looking young woman, she opens her mouth to comment but doesn't. "We have a reservation at seven. Jim is downstairs pacing. Let's go. Parking is never easy."

Le Mangoire, all Provence yellow, orange, and blue, opened eleven weeks ago and this weeknight is booked full, with boisterous groups of four and six seated outside while other customers mill around, waiting to get in.

As they approach, Margie squeals, pulling Annie to a halt and pointing through the window inside the eatery as Ismene barrels onward with Jim in tow toward the diminutive hostess, and says, "Hey, there's that good-looking roofer you told me about. See him? The one holding the camera?"

Puzzled, Annie asks, ". . .How do *you* know? You were never at the house when he was."

"Oh, Auntie and I bumped into him when we got you the sk—"

Annie's eyes open and she stares at her cousin. "Margie! Don't tell me this is a setup!"

"No, no." Margie exhales, then plunges into an explanation. "Well, not exactly. It happens to be your mother's birthday today." Doing her Ismene imitation, hand waving gracefully in the air, Margie continues, "But I can't say she wasn't *delighted* to find out that Andy—"

"Andy?"

"Yes, he asked me to call him Andy. Anyway, *Andy* is a friend of the owner, and he was happy to put in a word for us to get an almost impossible reservation as a favor because he's taking ad photos for the restaurant's tonight. Isn't that great?"

Annie purses her lips and remains silent.

"Oh, don't be such a martyr. If you're going to act so pigheaded, and you don't want him, I will *gladly* take him off your hands—he's really yummy." With that, Margie pushes ahead to join her aunt and her brother.

Now exasperated, Annie squares her shoulders and, plunging through the door in an attempt to catch up with her cousin, nearly collides with a waiter with a French accent. *"Pardon,"* he says. He's wearing black from head to toe and a long apron almost to the floor, and he flawlessly bobs around her with a tray of plates—one of *cas-*

soulet, another of duck *confit,* and a third of *moules aux pommes frites*—
the earthy smells of old-fashioned country cooking wafting by as he
moves past her.

Distracted by watching Ismene, in the distance, insisting the hostess seat them in the corner by the fireplace where a gas fire suggests
a romantic inn somewhere other than within city limits, and while
trying once more to get out of the waiter's way as he heads back into
the kitchen, Annie accidently backs into someone and turns to find
Andrew adjusting his tripod to take another shot.

"Ah, so sorry!" Annie tries to get away before he notices.

Still intent on switching one lens for another, he replies, "No
problem," without looking up. But the scent of gardenia wafts toward
him, which he now associates with only one person, and he does a
double take. "*Annie? Hi.*" He tries not to gape at the waif turned
swan.

"Oh, hi. I, ah, didn't know you were going to be here till, uh,
my cousin Margie told me just a minute ago."

"Boy, you clean up well."

"Um, yeah, thanks." She looks down at the floor, unable to meet
his eyes. "I guess it's a good thing I bumped into you, because I owe
you an apology. I want to say I'm sorry for saying you're not a gentleman."

"No need to apologize." Fiddling with his lens, he finally looks
up to meet her gaze and says, "I'm the one who needs to say I'm
sorry. Greene ticked me off. And you were right, as a result of losing
my temper, I *didn't* behave like a gentleman."

"Guess he made us both a bit crazy."

"Yeah. . . . You really do look great."

"I guess so. I mean," she says, blushing, "thanks. My mother's birthday...but you know that. She likes her guests to dress accordingly." Before she can stop herself, she adds, "Don't ever let her see you wearing shorts after 6:00 p.m. anywhere except in the backyard."

"Or wearing baseball hats."

They both laugh.

"Yeah, I saw Ismene's entrance here shake up the place. I was going to go over after this shot and wish her a happy birthday. Hey, where's your dad?"

Annie shakes her head. "He died when I was a little."

"Oh—sorry. I had no idea. It must be tough, especially on days like today."

Annie looks into his huge blue eyes and admits what she's never told another living soul. "The worst part is, I don't remember him. I mean, I was almost four when he died, but I don't remember him at all. Like I've wiped him completely from my life."

They stand in silence for a moment, and her curiosity finally gets the better of her. "You do this often?"

"This?" He holds up his camera. "As often as I can. If I'm ever lucky enough to retire, it will be to this. The camera gives me joy."

"You prefer photographing people?"

"Mostly. The human face is kinda fascinatingly complex. Though, for a friend, I'll shoot an interior scene or two. Hey, Ismene's waving at us—allow me." He tucks his equipment into the kitchen hallway, calls out to the owner chef, who nods, and offers his arm to Annie. With an embarrassed giggle, she takes it and allows him to navigate her through the maze of tables right to the back.

Ismene has already arranged for a bottle of champagne to be

opened, and five glasses are ready.

Jim, thankful for another male presence, reaches over and grabs Andrew's hand to introduce himself. "Saw you doing your stuff. Really impressive-looking camera. What have you got?"

"Hi, I'm—" and for a moment he looks at Annie before he replies—"I'm Andrew. Nice to meet you, too. It's a Nikon."

"What lens are you using?"

"Moderate wide angle, to shoot this scene."

"Ah, I hear a Canon EOS is a really cool camera."

Andrew shrugs. "For me it's not the camera, it's the lenses. I like the Nikon optics."

Ismene is growing impatient. "Andrew dear, will you make me happy and join us for dinner?"

"I'm working, unfortunately, but I would be happy to toast to the birthday girl." The five lift their glasses, and Andrew takes the lead: "To Ismene—may you always be a powerhouse, full of life, full of grace, always entertained and entertaining. Happy birthday."

The chorus of Happy Birthdays accompanying the clinking of glasses is very quickly interrupted when the group overhears a man behind them growl, "I *know* I reserved the table next to the fireplace for tonight."

Flustered, the hostess, throwing a sorrowful look at Ismene, says, "I'm sorry, sir, there must have been some mix up with the reservations. Please let me seat you at the banquette on the other side, and the house will buy you both a drink."

"Oh, look, Robert, it's Ismene and Annie Clairmont—old family *friends*. How lovely to see you again," Lara drawls, hanging on to Greene and behaving as if she has not spent the last five minutes watching all the players interact, noticing mostly the sparks between Annie and the young man, while Robert finally got the hostess's attention. Lara is in a gray silk dress that hugs her curves in just the right ways, blond hair swept into a chignon with one strand falling negligently to the side of her face to suggest the appropriate level of wantonness.

Robert, recognizing most of the gathered group, flushes, remains silent, and stands back while Lara disengages from his arm and puts her hand out as Ismene introduces first Jim, then Margie, and finally Andrew.

"I saw you taking pictures. You do this for a living?"

He shakes his head, grinning. "Wish I could." He quickly nods toward Greene to acknowledge his presence as he shakes the hand Lara has offered. A patron eager to get to the bathroom moves too quickly, and Lara bumps into Andrew, spilling his drink over the front of his shirt. A profusion of laughter and apologies follows.

Annie's jaw drops as she watches Lara brush her breast against Andrew's forearm, insisting he take her handkerchief to dry himself, which he accepts with a smile before making his way into the bathroom to dry off.

Once settled at a table, Greene orders two martinis, making sure the house uses the most expensive vodka they stock. He also wrangles a small, complimentary plate of *charcuterie* to go with it. Finally satisfied, martini in hand, he turns his attention to his guest, who tips her glass to his and takes a long sip. Setting the glass back down on the table, Lara is pleased to see a perfect replica of her lips in Jungle Red on it. While her cousin's eyes are riveted on her breasts, she considers her next question carefully. Leaning toward him, she asks in a conspiratorial voice, "So you have a secret plan to get elected mayor, have you?"

"Well," he chuckles knowingly, "it never hurts to be ready with Plan B," and takes another swallow.

She shrugs. "I don't know. Does anyone ever get elected on a platform of 'good' government anymore? Do people believe that's possible?"

He is about to protest, but she quickly adds, "Clearly no reflection on you, Robert. Your motivations are. . .crystal clear." She heaves a deep sigh calculated to thrust her breasts farther forward and watches his gaze follow their movement. She continues, "Surely it would be a shame if someone of your caliber didn't get into office."

Leaning back in his chair, arms folded, he assures her, "I'm getting a lot of feedback from people who are fed up with the status quo to back me and help me run my campaign. It's obvious who's the better candidate. Compare our education levels, our ages, even our outlook on life. I mean, the man is a dinosaur. In this day and age of health fanatics, he smokes *cigars*, of all things. And he certainly doesn't hit the gym four times a week like me."

Moving closer to this exotic creature, so she can get a better whiff of his pricy cologne, he flexes a bicep for Lara to touch. "I'm not some tired old man doing the same tired old thing. With due diligence and some effort, it might not be a landslide, but I'll do okay."

She moves a bit closer and whispers, "I've been hearing some *delicious* gossip from Aunt Harriet about a skull, and how the mayor may be running interference on behalf of—well, *others?*" She nods toward the Clairmont table, where the constant crescendos of laughter have been filling the room. "I mean, is that outrageous or what?"

ANNIE CAN'T HELP BUT TAKE A PEEK behind her to see how the Greene party is doing. They certainly seem cozy. Good. She remembers how Lara flirted with Andrew, and it makes her blood boil. Lara can't possibly be his type. She looks like a woman who takes for granted the attention she receives because of her looks. Annie pushes a medium-rare piece of steak from one side of the plate to the other.

Ismene implores her daughter, "Will you stop playing with your food as if you were nine?"

Ignoring this complaint, the young woman considers how Andrew didn't blush when Lara came onto him. Maybe he prefers women who are forward. Maybe he's used to them falling all over him. Didn't Mrs. Hill say he's had lots of girlfriends? Well, Annie concludes, as she waves the plate away when the French waiter inquires for a second time whether she is finished or not, it's clear that I'm not his type, and why would I care anyway? I certainly would not want to spend time with someone who is a player.

As dessert and coffee are being served—one candle on a lemon tart for Ismene to blow out—Andrew, in his black leather jacket and black fedora, and with equipment slung over his shoulder in two bags, makes his way back to their table to say good night. Ismene insists he draw up an extra chair and sit between her and her daughter to have a cup of coffee and some dessert with them.

He joins in the laughter as she regales them with a tale of going horseback riding for the first time, and how that skittish horse, out of control, raced pell-mell under a low tree branch, leaving her hanging from it.

Annie, unable to stop herself, asks Andrew while Margie and Jim tease Ismene about being up a tree, "Lara is a very beautiful woman, isn't she?"

"Yeah, she is, if you like that kind of look."

"And do you like that kind of look?"

"I know this sounds insane, but as far as I'm concerned, no matter how beautiful a woman is, if she doesn't have a firm handshake, she's going to be a lot more trouble than it's worth."

Before Annie can reply, he stands up to wish everyone a good night. Shaking hands with Jim, winking at Margie, he grabs Ismene's hand and kisses it, and pausing for a moment, not quite sure what to do, bends quickly to give Annie a kiss that eventually lands on her cheek but not before accidently brushing the side of her mouth. As he lopes out the door with his heavy bags, Annie's jaw drops for the second time in one night.

Book Two

1944

CHAPTER 7

G INNY SPENCER REPLACED THE PHONE in its cradle. It hadn't quite sunk in yet, what Bill's father had tried to stammer out before succeeding—that Bill was dead. Mr. Kaminski had said he would have preferred to come over to give her the news in person. The telephone was no proper way for her to find out, but he couldn't leave his wife alone just then. They would meet, however, sometime soon.

Silently thanking her dead father for having kept a well-stocked bar and wine cellar, Ginny made her way to the liquor cabinet and poured herself a double. She drifted to the dining room table, covered in ecru lace, sat down, and considered the pile of essays written by her fifth graders, mostly tediously labored, on what our forefathers had meant when they said we all have a right to life, liberty, and the pursuit of happiness. Bill's rights to any of these were certainly gone.

Blast it! She should have insisted, over his objections, that they get married before he went to England. Her heart, instead of being wrenched apart, was bursting full of love for the man she had met the first day of class at Teacher's College. Fresh-faced, with lots of freckles, he had turned, caught her eyes, and smiled as they both emerged from some lecture, and—though she hadn't known it at the time—she'd been smitten right then and there.

"Damn it," she muttered, "why can't I cry?" Is this what it's like for someone to be in shock? she wondered as she took another mouthful of whiskey.

She picked up one of the essays, grimaced, and tossed it down again. Bobby Ahearn had submitted the same essay his older sister had the year before. Something about the phrasing reminded Ginny of Harriet, who, conscious that she wasn't as pretty as some of the other girls and always wearing her sisters' hand-me-downs, compensated by being garrulous and expressing an exaggerated sense of civility. "May I please" and "if I may" peppered her conversation: a Jane Austen character in the making. Her favorite essay phrase, "I have observed," a plea to be taken seriously and doomed to fail, punctuated every other paragraph. The boy hadn't bothered to change his sister's wording one iota.

There was no point calling in the mother. With two sons fighting somewhere in the Pacific, the woman didn't need more to worry over. Tapping her red pencil against the table, Ginny decided there was another way to handle the matter. Fortunately, she was in the habit of saving things.

THE NEXT MORNING, GIGGLES ECHOED DOWN the red-brick and green-painted corridor as a number of students pushed against a glassed-in display showcasing the best essays produced by the children. Ginny had displayed both Ahearn papers side-by-side. Harriet—blinded by fury—shoved her way out of the crowd, yanking her younger brother by his elephantine ear, and ran straight into Miss Spencer with her brother flapping to and fro like laundry on a line. Before the girl opened her mouth, Ginny rumbled in her best Sunday-school-teacher voice, "I want to see you both after school," and strode off.

Five hours later, two disconcerted Ahearns took seats in the front row of Ginny's classroom. Ginny pulled up a chair and sat facing them. Harriet was about to plead on their behalf when Ginny said, "I don't care how Bobby got the essay, whether you gave him a copy of some previous draft you prepared, or he took it without your consent. It doesn't matter. Bobby either doesn't want to, or can't, do the work. Your mother has enough going on right now. You need to *help* Bobby do his homework. But not do it for him."

She turned to the truculent boy and barked, "Tomorrow during recess, you are going to write your own essay." He was crestfallen, and his sister was about to gloat when she added, "After school, you and your sister will go over it while I watch. Bobby, this will give you a chance to get something other than an 'F' for the essay you turned in. Harriet also gets a second chance to be of real help by putting her excellent writing skills to good use—*without* aiding and abetting an act of plagiarism. And in doing so, the two of you avoid getting hauled into the principal's office along with your mother."

WHEN GINNY GOT HOME, she opened her door to find a letter with a military postal code that had been slipped through the mail slot. Thinking it must be a mistake, she tore it open—only to find it had been sent by one of Bill's army buddies, a Sergeant Bud Crocker, who had served under him for the last ten months. Enclosed was a sealed letter from Bill.

Hardly able to keep her hands from trembling, she scanned the sergeant's letter, which explained that he had found the enclosed addressed to her among the lieutenant's things and wanted to get it to her as soon as possible without it being a shock, since she was bound to have already received the news of Bill's death. He went on to say that it had been an honor to serve under Bill, and that he was very sorry for her loss.

Without taking a breath, she inhaled the words in that familiar schoolboy handwriting:

> *You know, I'm not allowed to say much about anything on the day-to-day stuff that goes on here. I can tell you that I am well. Missing you desperately. Food is lousy—what I wouldn't give for some of Mom's perogies. Army life is a lot of hurry up and wait. We spend the waiting-around time swapping stories. Late at night, when it quiets down, most of us have a photograph or two that we stare at. Just know that your picture is the last one I look at. The one I took by the lake three years ago. Hair messed up, laughing, scolding me to stop as I tripped the shutter. It's amazing how you don't know how beautiful you are. How completely unaware that neither makeup nor a comb can really add a darn thing to how wonderful you look when you laugh—even if it's at me.*
>
> *All my love, Bill*

Then it hit, like a blow to her chest, that never again would she get a letter from him. All the tears that she hadn't been able to release for weeks poured out as if some emotional dam had burst her heart. She was soon on the floor sobbing.

She woke up in that position and heaved herself upright. Glancing through the parlor window, she saw that a clear night had fallen, made her way into the kitchen, and pulled out some leftover borscht Bill's mother had taught her to make. Putting the flame on low, she read and reread the letter as if each subsequent time was the first, searching for something that she had missed earlier.

She shivered, remembered the soup, and ladled some into a bowl. The horrible sense of being completely alone blanketed her as she sat at the maple harvest table, listening to the absence of any noise in her home or out. She thought about the first time silence had frightened her. Her mother had died when she was seven, Grace fourteen, and Betty sixteen. Raised by Patricia, their Negro housekeeper, and her father, a dedicated physician who, disappointed at having had a third daughter, had raised her more like a son. When he followed her mother in death the year before, there had been no way she dared shed a tear lest she disappoint him. Grace, who had been Mother's favorite, and Betty, who had been Father's, were inconsolable at his death, but they had long ago flown the coop. Married with children, they had less time to spare being involved in the day-to-day care of a sick old man.

Having taken care of the elderly for decades, Father had refused any kind of treatment, swearing he'd rather drop dead suddenly than have a long, painful decline forcing him to be nursed or, worse, turned into a damn baby.

"Horse feathers!" he'd shout at any attempt to reason with him. "I'm not a sick man, just an old one! Getting old is as natural as, well, as giving birth. And the last time I checked, trying to interfere with that was illegal in this country. Only a fool thinks you can cheat death out of its due. And anyone who tries more than likely lives to regret it."

Desperate, hungry for more news of Bill, she grabbed a piece of paper and, having searched for the sergeant's name in his letter, wrote:

> *Dear Mr. Crocker,*
>
> *Thank you for your kindness. I am sure Bill is not the first comrade you have lost. But I do appreciate that you took the time to send me his letter. It's hard to explain, however, that though I was his fiancée, in some ways, he was also my best friend. I miss him terribly.*
>
> *I'm sure you have family and friends and have no need of dealing with a grieving woman, but if you don't mind the intrusion I would like to send you a letter from time to time to keep in touch?*
>
> *Cordially,*
>
> *Ginny Spencer*

CHAPTER 8

RUDY HANDELMAN WAS ONLY TEN, but he was a man in love. Because he was sickly with asthma, his mother kept him home a great deal. Rudy considered this fortuitous, since it fell upon the beauteous Miss Spencer to keep him from lagging behind in classwork. That she lived across the street was a special bonus. Besides his having the joy of going to her home every day he missed school, she had graciously offered him the opportunity to call upon her if he needed help with some sticky math problem. Since he hated math and had no head for it, opportunities to visit abounded. His mother, and sister who took Mother's cue, babied him, but Miss Spencer made him feel grown-up by offering him cups of tea in nice china and even a cookie or two when he called upon her for help in homework. She had taught him to love poetry by lending him her copy of *A Treasury of the Familiar*.

She didn't laugh at him as the other boys did because he couldn't play ball as well as they could. Instead, if he happened to wander over to say hello while she was on her knees working in the garden, she'd hand him a second hand-rake, and they'd clear the backyard of weeds in no time. All the while she would point out what was growing or about to burst forth and flower, and why she loved this plant or that bush. All talk about color, shape, vibrancy...and depth. He'd listen, hoping the conversation, and work in the garden, would never ever stop.

Miss Spencer was the one person he knew in the whole world who had depth, so it was killing him to see her so sad about her fiancé having died. Rudy grudgingly remembered him as an okay guy even though he had competed for and won Miss Spencer's affection. Rudy now felt ashamed, thinking of all the times he had pretended to have a rifle, which he'd silently aim at his rival's heart from his bedroom window on the second floor, and pull the trigger every time Bill Kaminski rang Miss Spencer's doorbell.

But since she got the terrible news just when school started, her heart had not been in tutoring or gardening. Even her waves and hellos from across the street, if they happened to meet, seemed not really there. It was not like her for leaves to be on the ground for so long around her home. Miss Spencer—unlike Dad and every other neighbor on the street who grumbled while tending to this chore— seemed to dance with the leaves as they whirled around her, a kaleidoscope of color in motion.

Rudy grabbed his blue sweater and cap and slipped out the back door as quietly as he could, hoping to elude his mother's usual litany of where and what and who. He slipped into the garage, grabbed the rake, and ran as fast as he could across the street, ignoring the game of stickball being played farther down by the neighborhood kids and the yells erupting to urge him to join them to even up the teams. Instead he parked himself under the maple tree, hesitated only for a moment, thinking about a long conversation he had had with her about tulips and roses, and weighing that against the risk of appearing pushy by performing this task unasked. He carefully drew the rake across the lawn, taking satisfaction in hearing it scratch against the hard earth, the dried leaves crackling as they moved about. In fact, he was enjoying himself so much that he didn't see Miss Spencer pulling up in her driveway in her light-blue Packard.

"Rudy, what possessed you to start raking *here?* I'm sure your father would be happy to have your help." Standing next to the low box hedge that bordered her front lawn, arms filled with schoolwork, Ginny peered at the funny little boy humming "Maple Leaf Rag" as he danced around the yard.

Grinning, he sang out, "Tulips and roses, Miss Ginny, tulips and roses."

It took her a moment to grasp what he was talking about, but then, for the first time in a *very* long while, she broke into a grin.

HARRIET AHEARN HADN'T APPRECIATED the way Miss Spencer treated her, allowing her no say in the whole mess—all because her brother had been too lazy to change her essay. Trudging off to school, she blurted out to no one in particular, "I've never been so humiliated!" She'd heard her mother more than once talk about how uppity the Spencers were. So polite, so correct, so nothing to fault. Of course not! They had money, and money meant position! Harriet kicked a rock, narrowing her green eyes; she was willing to bet if *Miss, Ginny, Spencer* had had to wear *her* sisters' hand-me-downs, hardly anyone would have taken notice because they were the best clothes for the best people. Harriet caught up with the hapless rock and was about to kick it again when she spied goody-two-shoes Rudy Handelman, the teacher's pet, and decided he was a far better target than the rock.

"Hi, Rudy. Can I—that is, *may* I—walk with you?" She smiled sweetly.

"Uh, sure, if you want to." They walked in silence, unsure of what to say to one another. Whether it was because they were both ten or because they came from different sides of town—making the gulf between them seem too wide—it was only when the children were half a block from the school yard that Rudy suddenly stopped short, staring at the sky.

"What are you doing?"

"Looking up at the trees." The boy having barely glanced at Harriet as he answered made her furious.

One hand on her hip and the other balancing her books she snapped, "I can *see that*."

"No—just look, will ya? The sky is different, all broken up by the branches. It looks—" he hesitated before finishing— "it looks romantic."

"Where did you get *that* idea?" she barked, imitating her mother when she lost her patience with one of her children.

"Miss Spencer."

"Ha, I knew it had to be something stupid like that."

"Miss Spencer is not stupid. Take that back."

Harriet's eyes narrowed once more. Seeing her chance, she swiveled her hips as she taunted Rudy by repeating, "*Miss* Spencer is *stupid, Miss* Spencer is *stupid, Miss* Spencer is *stupid.*"

"Stop it! That's not *nice.*"

"*Miss* Spencer is *stupid, Miss* Spencer is *stupid—*"

"You're being really mean. *Stop* it," Rudy pleaded.

"*Miss* Spencer is *stupid, Miss* Spencer is—"

Furious at the senseless cruelty, he shouted back, "*You're* the one who's stupid. You wouldn't know what romantic is if it hit you on the *head!*"

"Mrs. Donovan," the girl squealed as she ran into the school yard as the children were lining up to enter the school and begin their day. "Mrs. Donovan, Rudy called me stupid! He called me stupid six *times*, Mrs. Donovan. He's so mean!"

RUDY HAD TRIED TO EXPLAIN HIMSELF to the principal. How Harriet had started it by calling Miss Spencer names. That she'd lied about his having called her stupid six times. It was the other way around. But the more he tried to tell the truth, the deeper in trouble he got. Now it was three o'clock, the classroom was empty, and Miss Spencer sat silently at her desk, correcting papers while he wrote, for the sixty-seventh time, *I will not call anyone stupid.*

Fifteen minutes later, cheeks flushed, he turned in the paper. He was trying to creep away without being noticed when he heard Miss Spencer call out, "Rudy, I heard what happened. I'm sorry you got in trouble defending me."

He forced himself not to look up, fighting the tears that were beginning to fill his eyes. "It's just not fair. Harriet was calling you names, Miss Spencer, but I got in trouble. Mrs. Donovan didn't even *listen* to me. She *always* thinks that it's the boys who are trouble-makers, not the girls."

Ginny bit her lower lip and shook her head. "Sometimes, Rudy, life is just not fair."

He shot a quick glance at her before looking down at the floor again. "Yes, ma'am," he replied, "but I still think looking at the sky through tree branches *is* romantic, even if Miss-Know-It-All Harriet Ahearn thinks it's stupid."

Ginny shut her grade book. "Is that what all this fuss was about, Rudy?"

Unable to speak, he nodded.

"I see." Drumming her finger absently on the desk, she tried to decide how to explain the obvious to a ten-year-old. "Rudy, not all people are the same. I am not suggesting one way is better than another. But some folks are more comfortable with what's concrete. You know—the everyday world that they see, hear, taste, touch, and smell. So when others are drawn to the intangible, which makes no sense to them, they can become furious, envious. . .and even hurtful. Why they get mean—well, that's not your concern for the moment. They are God's creatures, too. But don't let anyone change your mind about how you see the world. It's not an easy way to live, Rudy, but you'll never go wrong if you keep true to yourself."

Glassy-eyed, he finally looked up, voice thick with the phlegm. "It gets lonely."

"I know, Rudy." Ginny smiled at the little boy before her and added, "I surely do know. But that's why we read poetry, listen to music, or walk in nature, so we know we're not alone."

A half hour later, as she approached her front door, Ginny herself looked up at the sky feeling the end of Indian summer closing in. She left the children's work, which still needed to be corrected, on the table in the hallway, hung up her navy jacket in the hall closet, and rushed to the dining room table to finish her letter to Sergeant Buddy Crocker.

CHAPTER 9

S EVENTEEN-YEAR-OLD SYLVIA AHEARN laid the letter down on the bed beside her. She lit a cigarette. Fortunately, her two sisters, with whom she shared the bedroom, were both downstairs arguing about whose turn it was to do the ironing—Harriet as usual, whining the most. This had allowed Sylvia to slip upstairs unnoticed for at least ten minutes, to reread Bud's letter. Ma would be back from work soon, and her sisters would scatter like mice rather than risk hearing her threats about turning them all out on the street for being stupid, lazy cows. Still, there was enough time to sneak a cigarette and think. She opened both windows—pulling back tattered lace curtains—and blew out the smoke, waving it on its way.

She had always dreamed, in those very few isolated moments to herself, of getting the hell out of the house, her family, and the life she saw herself doomed to—shanty Irish filled with screaming, cursing, drinking, children and more children, and finally, of course, church. Had seen her chance when she read an ad in the paper and begged Mom to allow her to volunteer at the USO in Times Square months before. Had somehow managed to wrangle a "yes" during a rare sentimental moment when her mother was thinking about her brothers Richie and John, and off she had gone into New York—a magical, bigger-than-life world. She'd lied about her age to become a USO junior hostess. While she was serving doughnuts, she had already noticed Bud standing in line, waiting his turn. He was different from the rest of the boys, who were mostly ruffians—seemed soft-spoken, polite, even a little shy, and most definitely *not* Catholic: her ticket out of a dreary life, and a very handsome one at that.

She blew more smoke out the window, stubbed out the cigarette, and looked down the street to see whether her mother was on the way. She didn't like Bud's letter. He went on and on about the funny coincidence that his dear dead friend's fiancée, Ginny Spencer, just happened to live in the same town that she did. He kept asking if she knew this person, or that person, Ginny knew. Which meant Ginny Spencer was moving in on her territory, and Sylvia didn't like that, not one bit.

She glanced at the letter once more, grimacing as she reread Bud's suggestion that perhaps she might want to get together with Ginny, since they had so much in common.

She picked up her pen and carefully considered how she was going to finish her letter.

Darling, it gets so lonely at night. I read your letters again and again, but I can hardly fall asleep just thinking about being in your arms. I miss you so much. If meeting Ginny Spencer makes you happy, I'll look her up right away.

She ran to the dresser, grabbed her Lantern Red lipstick, and outlined her lips just as she'd learned from the girl at the drugstore counter, making sure the color on her upper lip extended beyond her natural line into a very full shape, and then doing the same on her lower lip. She smacked the lips together to make sure the red was evenly distributed, then pressed them to the bottom of the letter, where they left a perfect imprint. Grinning at the impression they left, she reached for her cologne, Tabu, which Bud had been sweet enough to buy her after she dropped a well-placed hint, and touched a drop of it to the letter before sealing it up quickly in the envelope, to make sure that when he opened the letter, the memory of her having first placed the scent between her breasts rather than behind her ears lingered long and hard.

Then she wrote a note to Ginny Spencer, asking her to meet the following Saturday at Minetti's for an ice cream. It was time to get a look at the competition. She would save herself a stamp by getting Harriet to give it to her after class.

GINNY BREEZED INTO MINETTI'S, which was crowded for a Saturday afternoon with people gathered for ice cream, newspapers, candy, sodas, and cigarettes. She spotted a pretty young woman with Harriet's coloring, wearing an outrageous hat. Clearly the hat—fire-engine red—was an attempt at looking grown up, which was comical and endearing at the same time.

"You must be Sylvia." Ginny offered her hand as she continued, "I am so pleased to meet you. Bud's letters are full of talk about you."

Sylvia regally extended her hand insofar as to come into partial contact with the other's. She had once read in a magazine that it was not ladylike for a woman to have too strong a handshake. As they sat down at one of the tables, she smiled sweetly. "His letters mention you quite a lot, too."

At the other end of the bustling room, in the meantime, Harriet had come in earlier to stake out some corner and watch her sister and teacher meet, hoping there'd be fireworks. She had steamed open Sylvia's letter, just as she'd seen her mother do when Pop got letters that were addressed only to him. And it'd worked just fine. The meeting was something she wouldn't have missed for the world, especially if Sylvia decided to make one of her scenes; it would be worth the wait.

Rudy had also entered the store, to get some candy with his weekly allowance, earned for doing chores around the house. As he considered his choices, he noticed Harriet peeking from behind the corridor that led to the bathroom. She kept sticking her head up past the half wall, then ducking back down. It was such odd behavior that he was standing there, mouth open, when Harriet finally noticed him. "What are you *staring* at?" she hissed.

"You! You're—"

"Get over here before they notice."

"Notice what? Who are you—"

Harriet grabbed him by the sleeve and pulled him into the corridor where she'd been hiding. "Ginny Spencer and my sister, you idiot. They're sitting at the table over there in the corner. They're both in love with the same man!"

"In *love*? How would *you* know?"

Harriet glared at the thick-headed boy. Turning up her nose, she coldly replied, "A woman *just knows*." Before he could comment, she punched him in the stomach, warning him to keep quiet.

At the other end of the soda shop, having gotten their ice cream placed before them, Sylvia offered Ginny a cigarette, which she declined. Sylvia shifted in her seat in order to appear considerate, blowing cigarette smoke up. "It must be so terrible to lose a loved one."

Ginny winced briefly and nodded.

"I'm so scared that I could lose Buddy."

While Sylvia had said this purely for effect, the sudden realization of someone's else's mortality at risk immediately reminded her of her own and created such a jolt that, before she could stop herself, she blurted, "And I'm scared to death if he comes back, too."

Ginny was at a loss for words.

At this point, there was no going back to acting the part of the lady, so Sylvia played her cards straight. "You wouldn't understand what it's like to grow up like me. You come from a *fine* family. There are things you would take for granted, that you think everybody knows. But they don't!"

She wiped her eyes with her hand, giving her time to recover from her moment of weakness. "Good thing Buddy's family is in Oklahoma. What would they think if they laid eyes on mine?" She spat out the next words. "People with no couth, no desire to better themselves." She took a drag from her cigarette. "Look, I need to make sure I get on his family's good side—to hide where I come from."

As Ginny considered this for a moment, poking at the dish of peach ice cream with her spoon, she mused quietly, "Buddy doesn't strike me as someone who would care about such things. I'm sure you would be welcomed into the family with open arms."

Sylvia shook her head and asked, "But will they *stay* open? For that, I need a certain amount of polish. The magazines tell you what a lady is supposed to do, but not how to do it, not really. You can teach me. I learn real fast when I want to."

When Ginny didn't immediately respond, the girl pleaded, "Besides, it would be a good excuse for us to spend time together. Wouldn't Buddy be just tickled to hear that we've become close, like two sisters? What do you say?"

CHAPTER 10

SALVATORE SAMARTINO HAD MISSED being drafted into the war by two years and hated it. He was proud to have become an American citizen, and the thought that he would not be able to protect the country that he had learned to love was a blow to his pride. While Americans never seemed to remember that they, too, had once come from somewhere else, the townspeople had slowly allowed him his place among them as the number of good-morning and good-evening nods to and from home accumulated, one at a time.

Besides, it crushed his sense of manhood to be thought of as too old go to war. A butcher, he was strong as an ox with large forearms and hands, tall, straight-backed, and far more muscular than a lot of younger men who sat at a desk all day at work.

His wife Angela, however, generally prone to speaking in soothing tones, became impossible whenever he mentioned anything about serving in the war. While coaxing a marinara sauce into being, she had once shouted, "Let Europe, in all her glory, go to hell!" When hunger forced her family to leave their home in Calabria, Angela had sworn she'd never become sentimental about a place that could not feed its own people.

But whatever she felt about the old country didn't stop her from sending socks and scarves to the neighborhood boys fighting overseas, and saving a portion of her oil and butter rations to make them cookies. Or going to early morning mass to light a candle and ask the Madonna to look after those young men placed in harm's way because of age-old border disputes nursed into a frenzy by soulless politicians.

Salvatore shook his head, thinking about the force of nature he had married. He'd finished unloading the week's delivery, which was not as much as had been expected. He sighed; his boss, unable to brave the silent, disappointed women faced with few or no choices at the counter, placed him more often than not behind it. Having learned a trick or two back in the old country about stretching what one had in lean times, Salvatore had convinced the boss, a grumpy German, to allow him to make sausages that replaced some meat and fat with potatoes, fennel seeds, and hot spices. The shop was developing a following, so that Salvatore had become much sought-after for his sausage-and-pepper recipe by housewives with German, English, and Irish last names.

Christina Hill sauntered into the shop, wrapped in a navy swing coat and matching beret jauntily tilted forward on her bright yellow hair. Once a dancer with the Rockettes, now happily married, she was almost as tall as he was and as easy-going as a summer breeze. "Hi, Sal. What you got for me today?"

"Same I got for you every day, Mrs. Christina, *nothing!*"

They laughed at their tired joke. Christina bought some pork and reached over the spotless counter to hand him money and a red ration coupon. Sal handed back some silver coins as well as two red tokens in change. Then she placed two cans with rendered fat on the counter and waited until she was reimbursed for her efforts.

At that moment, the bell tinkled, the glass door opened, and Salvatore was startled to see his eldest son, Giovanni, stomp in, his left eye blackened and his nose bloodied.

"What *happened?*" Sal exclaimed. "Who *did* this to you?"

The twelve-year-old swallowed and wiped his nose on the sleeve of his brown jacket. "Two boys called me a *guinea*, Pappa, when we was walking home from school. I decked them good, but it was two against one. They made fun of me for having a Eye-ta-*lee*on name. Why can't I have an *American* name like. . .like John? They're always making fun of me cause of my stupid name. Then they said Mamma has a moustache. I don't even know what they are talkin' about! Mamma don't have no moustache!" He stood there glaring up at his father.

Salvatore shook his head. "Giovanni, what did I tell you? I do not want you talking like a hoodlum. It is not 'Mamma don't have no moustache,' it is 'Mamma does not have a moustache.' And you say, 'We *were* walking home,' not 'We was.' I spent hours and hours, late at night, reading many books, so I can speak English well. Speak like a gentleman, and you *are* a gentleman. Of *course* Mamma has no moustache. She is the most beautiful woman I know. And you were born here, so you are an American no matter what your name is."

"But I want to be like everybody else. I want to call you, 'Dad' and you to call me 'John.' I don't want to be so. . . so Eye-ta-*lee*on.

Then they'll beat up the Greek boy, Stavros, instead of me."

The father and Christina exchanged glances. She cleared her throat. "Perhaps there could be a compromise?"

The boy's eyes widened, "What is it, Mrs. Christina? Oh, *please*, what?"

"Well, I always thought that Giovanni sounded a lot like Johnny, and Pop a lot like Pappa."

Salvatore dismissed the suggestion with a wave of a hand. "No offense, Mrs. Christina, you are a kind woman, but is that any way to show a father respect? Call him a soda?"

"Oh, please, please, *please*, Pappa. I promise, when no one is listening, to call you Pappa instead of Pop. But *please* can I go by Johnny? They'll probably think it's sissy for someone as old as me, but it's better than nothing." He snuffled and waited with cap in hand.

"Okay, son, maybe. We will talk some more about it when I come home."

The child already knew he'd got his way from the defeated look on his father's face. "Oh, *thank* you, Pops—well, anyway, thank you. And thank you, too, Mrs. Christina." He grabbed her hand with both of his and shook it vigorously. "You're the best."

He was already gone when his father thought to shout after him, "We still have to talk about *fighting*."

Christina laughed. "A little spoiling once in a while doesn't do any harm, Sal."

Again the bell on the door tinkled; this time Margaret Ahearn marched into the shop, worn black purse swung up against her chest like a shield, demanding, "Are you *that* kid Giovanni's father?" Before

Salvatore could open his mouth, she barreled on, "Your son took a couple of swings at my boys, James and Peter Ahearn. We, in this here country, are civilized. Your son's got a lot of nerve going around trying to beat up kids! What are you going to do about it?" She stood there, shoulders squared, scowling.

The butcher wiped his hands before addressing the irate woman. "I am Salvatore Samartino, Gio—Johnny's father." When the woman remained silent, he continued, "My son just left the store. He told me that two boys made fun of him and his mother. Tonight I will speak to him about fighting, Mrs. Ahearn. But boys fight. Sometimes it is good not to interfere. Better to let them work it out. No? But these boys, *your* two boys, said something untrue about Johnny's mother. And my son fought back, even if it was an unfair fight, two against one."

He waited for his words to sink in, and for this angry woman to offer something, anything, in return.

Instead, her eyes narrowed, she addressed Christina. "These little foreign brats know nothing about being American."

Tilting her head to return the angry woman's gaze, Christina paused before replying, "I'm able to trace my people back to the Revolution, Margaret. But if I remember right, both your grandmother and father spoke with a brogue. Was a time not so long ago when *Irish Need Not Apply* was a common sign around these parts."

Red-faced and with nostrils flaring, Margaret opened and shut her mouth twice. She finally found her voice and shouted at Salvatore, "Are you going to do something about your son, or do I have to go to the police?"

"Mrs. Ahearn, I will speak to my son about fighting. But he already knows that no real man ever insults a woman, because that is not civilized. I think this is true in Italy and is true in America." Her finger punctuated every word. "You got a lot of nerve thinking you are better than me, mister, cause you're not." She reached for the door, adding over her shoulder, "Better watch what you buy here, Christina. I wouldn't put it by *this* one—" she yanked her chin in Salvatore's direction—"to sell horse meat or *worse* in those sausages of his."

GINNY SMILED WHENEVER SHE SAW one of Buddy's letters in the mail. He always managed to recall some story about Bill during the nine months they had spent side by side, which in turn allowed her to write back and reminisce. This kept Bill close, and in the meantime she had begun to like this young man for who he was.

She opened the letter, quickly scanned it, and left it on the demilune table that had been there since before her father was born in that home. Glancing at the grandfather clock, she realized she was late and made her way deliberately into the kitchen to pull out shortening, flour, eggs, sugar, baking soda, cream of tartar, and cinnamon, along with the recipe, carefully rewritten on an index card, for snickerdoodles. She thought it might be fun to bake a family recipe with Sylvia, as well as show her how to put together a tea table. She took out a pink hemstitched linen cloth and spread it on the kitchen table, a lace doily for the tray, and found the rose-embroidered napkins, which she started to touch up with an iron when she heard the back door creak open.

Sylvia came through the scuffed white door, unannounced and breathless. She had left her mother apoplectic about running off for etiquette lessons without having done her share of the day's chores. Something about placing etiquette where the sun didn't shine had been hurled as a parting volley as Sylvia ran out of bellowing range and made her way across town to the "hillside" section.

"Just in time. Why don't you put the kettle on?"

Sylvia obliged her, putting enough water for two cups into the beat-up copper kettle.

"Oh, more than *that*, Sylvie," Ginny coaxed, using her pet name for the girl, which she'd noticed blunted any resentment Sylvia was quick to unleash against any perceived criticism. "We girls like our tea." Ginny smiled in satisfaction as she placed the ironed napkins, cups and plates, sugar and creamer, in their designated spots on the table.

The kettle whistle sang, and Sylvia, taking her cue, carefully poured a bit of boiling water into the pot to warm it, then poured it out. In went three tea bags and the rest of the boiling water to steep under a snug sunflower cozy. While the oven worked its way to 350 degrees, all the measured ingredients were quickly mixed together and the dough dropped on prepared cookies sheets.

Ginny had soon fished the teabags out of the earthen pot and set them aside to be used one more time for her early morning cup. They poured their first, waiting for the cookies to finish. The tea steamed in blue-and-white Staffordshire. Ginny glanced out the kitchen window. The winter sun showed no promise of spring. But was it her imagination, or were the trees and bushes beginning to blush the faintest pink?

Warm cookies finally took their place on another piece of Staffordshire. Sylvia bit into one of her cookies—the first she'd ever baked—eyes bright with pride. "They're really good!"

There was something childlike in her hunger to learn about Ginny's family. She laughed so hard she barely could catch her breath as Ginny recalled a time when the whole household was in an uproar over a mouse. The family cat, Midnight Blue, had a habit of catching field mice and bringing them home as gifts. One night, however, bored with chasing the petrified mouse herself, she dropped it on the pillow by Aunt Violet's face. Father's sister had come to visit for a week, and the piercing screams had brought the entire family to her room. Midnight Blue perched on the windowsill, watching intently as Father and three girls scrambled about, hollering to one another as each took a turn attempting to scoop the mouse into a small bowl while the others struggled to block its escape. When Father finally caught it, he refused to kill it as Aunt Violet demanded, mumbling something about God's creatures, and, wearing only his pajamas and a robe, walked to the park at the end of the street at two a.m. to release the mouse into quieter surrounds.

Sylvia wiped tears from her eyes. She hated to admit it, but she liked Ginny more than she cared to. "What are we going to do tomorrow?"

"Ah. Tomorrow I tutor a little boy, so how about the following day we make some soup? How about potato and leek?"

"Potato and leek," repeated Sylvia. "Doesn't sound so fancy."

"Yes, but if you add some cream to it, then it becomes vichyssoise, a very elegant French soup that can be served cold."

"Cold? Who ever heard of a cold soup? The French are really crazy. Anyway, will ya...I mean, will you *please* excuse me?" Sylvia hopped up from the table and kept repeating *vee-shee-swa* on her way to the bathroom upstairs.

Ginny shook her head; at this rate she would go through a week's worth of butter in two days. It would be tight this week. She wouldn't have as many ration stamps to leave at the grocer's for those who needed them much more than she did. It couldn't be helped.

Sylvia was sashaying down the stairs humming "It's Love Love Love" when she noticed the opened letter. "Sorry," she yelled toward the kitchen, "I forgot to turn off the water upstairs." Shutting the door behind her, she read the letter. They sounded so chummy. Buddy never talked to *her* about books or about politics. Did he think *she* was *stupid?* She was about to rip up the letter but got a hold of herself. She was *not* stupid, no sir. Even Ma always said that of the lot of them, it was she who had a head on her shoulders. "Damn it, Sylvia," Ma'd scream, "if you weren't so lazy, you could make something of yourself."

Then she remembered that she was jealous of Ginny Spencer and of her fine house and oh-so-fine family. She remembered that Bud was closer to Ginny in age. She remembered that she had too many siblings, not enough money, and needed to get out of the life she saw as a trap. And that Ginny, no matter how many tea parties they had together, was the only thing standing in her way. But Sylvia needed her rival for now. To learn all she could and prove she was better than someone old enough—well, almost old enough—to be a spinster. Picking up the letter, she looked in the mirror. Cheeks flushed, nose red, she took a breath, splashed cold water on her face, and closed the door behind her, humming "I'll Get By" as she dropped the letter where she had found it. When she approached the table, she sat down without a word.

Ginny noticed the change. "Sylvie, is everything all right?"

"Ah-huh."

The silence continued as they sipped more tea.

"Say—you have any books you think I should be reading?"

"What kind of book do you want to read?"

"Love poems especially. So I can think of Buddy, my own true love." Sylvia glanced at the other woman to see if this bothered her in any way. No matter how hard she tries, thought Sylvia, Ginny won't be able to hide her feelings for Buddy from me.

Ginny smiled. "I think I can lend you a book or two. Sure it won't make you too sad that you are apart?"

CHAPTER 11

SALVATORE WAS STANDING OUTSIDE the front door to his tiny cape cottage, which managed to house two adults and two boys very well besides allowing his wife to grow the vegetables and herbs that she considered essential for feeding a family. His boys didn't mind sharing a room. Bedtime echoed with sounds of shouting, laughter, and argument. All that fuss was music to Salvatore's ears—proof of a happy home.

Combined with Angela's cooking and baking—particularly her bread and rolls hot out of the oven, slathered with butter when they had it or margarine when they didn't—it was no wonder that, as soon as the tray was placed on the counter to cool, neighborhood children appeared out of nowhere, gathered on the back stoop and hoping to get a taste, from the moment the crocuses emerged to well after the first winter frost.

He opened the door, removing his brown fedora, to find little Joey demanding, with his chubby hand fashioned into a gun, that Johnny stick-em-up. Johnny, who had already played this scene several times for his little brother, grabbed his chest, hurled himself to the floor, and solemnly announced, "I'm dead." Opening one eye to look at his sibling he added, "This time for good!"

At the sight of their father, both instantly left Main Street in Tombstone to hurl themselves at him, each demanding to be hugged first.

It wasn't till after dinner, when the boys were getting ready for bed, that Angela asked why he was so quiet.

"We hardly get by on what I make, Angela. I need to do more. I don't imagine I will become a rich man, but it's hard to watch you make do with so little."

"I'm not interested in being rich, *mio amore*," Angela whispered, wrapping her arm around her husband's shoulder as she kissed his head. She then placed two cups of coffee on the kitchen table and sat down facing him. "And, really, there is no reason to worry, for I have been putting away money for a very long time."

"Yes, yes, I know about your knitting bag."

Angela's eyebrows arched as she shot a look at her husband.

Raising his hands to avoid a quarrel about privacy, he quickly added, "I went to use one of your needles to open a box. . . . That money is yours to do as you wish, Angela. What I want is the boys should go to college—and become whatever they want, but respectable."

"I've seen too many respectable people with hearts as black as coal. Is that what you want our boys to learn?"

"No. Never. But I want them to have the choice that we didn't have, Angela. To help them go to college, I will take work from time to time on the weekend."

RUDY KNOCKED AT THE DOOR Saturday morning and waited for Miss Spencer to answer it. Although it was a bright, almost spring-like day, he didn't feel sunny and was less than enthusiastic when she greeted him.

The two sat at the dining room table, working their way through one division problem after another. In time, laying his pencil down, the boy sighed and looked away.

"Rudy, you've barely said two words. It's not like you."

"I know, Miss Spencer, but I'm really sad, 'cause you're going to leave me—I mean leave us."

"Leave? Whatever gave you that idea?"

"Well—" he shrugged, then continued without making eye contact—"when girls fall in love, don't they get married, and move away, and start families?"

"Yes, sometimes. Do you. . .what makes you think that I am doing that any time soon?"

"Harriet Ahearn!" Rudy scowled, involuntarily placing his hand on his abdomen at the thought of his tormentor. "At Minetti's, I saw her hiding behind a wall. She pulled me over, saying that you and her sister Sylvia were in love with the same man. When I asked her how she knows that, *she* said that '*a woman knows.*'" The tips of the boy's ears flushed red. "Before I could tell her she was full of soap, she punched me, told me to be quiet, and to watch the two of you eating ice cream! She left mad that you didn't start fighting."

Ginny rubbed her face with her hands, elbows on the table. "You don't say 'left mad,' you say 'left angry.'"

Rudy imitated his teacher by also placing elbows on the table to hold his head up. "Aw, Miss Spencer, Harriet tells a lot of stories.

But I got to thinking, even if Harriet got it wrong again, how long before this fella comes to his senses and sees how wonderful you are? And then you will be gone, and this whole town will become boring as hell."

"Rudy!"

"Sorry, ma'am. But I'd. . .I'd miss working with you in the garden—"

"Child, I'm not going anywhere."

The boy pursed his lips and kept silent.

"Rudy, I am *not*. Do you understand me?"

Though he didn't look up to meet his teacher's eyes, he offered a hesitant, "Yes, ma'am."

"Good!" But neither was fully convinced that anything at that moment had been settled for good. Ginny was shaken by having been spied upon. And Rudy believing, no matter what she told him, that she was bound to leave him sooner or later for this imaginary lover, didn't help matters either.

Smiling bravely, Ginny suggested, "I think we could both use a cup of tea. How about some snickerdoodles, too?"

When she shut the door an hour later, Ginny had a splitting headache. Dad had always said that *noblesse oblige* only counted when it was difficult to follow through. If one was helping out for the wrong reasons, like feeding one's pride, the intention was a cheat bound to confound the situation and insure that no one walked away clean.

The Ahearns were testing her patience at the very least. Irritated, she scrubbed the teacups, saucers, and plates with far more zeal than necessary. It occurred to her that maybe she wasn't as much of a lady as she imagined.

She didn't feel like cooking dinner and made herself a ham sandwich instead. She took a half-hearted bite. The sandwich tasted like sand. Grabbing some mustard from the refrigerator to spark up both the sandwich and her appetite, she took another bite and nearly choked on the mustard.

She reviewed her options in the present situation: a girl, a mere slip of a thing, considering her a romantic rival competing for Buddy's attention. There was no way to directly address the situation without making things worse. Any assurances on Ginny's part would immediately become suspect.

Having replaced the sandwich on the plate, she startled herself by asking, *Am* I in love with Buddy? She'd never had to ask that about Bill. But Bill was not here. Neither, technically, was Buddy, fighting overseas. But she had to confess that she'd be lying if she didn't admit that her heart raced just a bit when she saw one of Buddy's letters.

For a while she sat staring at the nearly untouched sandwich before it occurred to her to ask, "How did I get myself in this mess?" There was no point being angry with anyone but herself. To have become an object of speculation, theater for the small-minded, was downright uncomfortable. Father had always laid a great store on probity. He believed those who had been blessed with certain advantages should be present, helpful, kind to others who were not so fortunate. He had counseled his daughter to take responsibility for her behavior, which meant clearly understanding her motives in any situation, and had warned her about making snap judgments about people. "If you haven't walked in their shoes, you can't judge," he'd remind her, looking up from under those bushy gray eyebrows of his, glasses perched on the tip of his nose, "And if you *have* walked in their shoes, you most certainly have no right to judge them."

THE NEXT DAY AFTER WORK, SHE LAID on the kitchen counter four potatoes, two fat leeks, and some parsley, and waited for her student.

Sylvia, without hesitation, came through the kitchen door. The two locked eyes.

Ginny had unwittingly adopted her best schoolmarm voice to say, "Have a seat, Sylvia."

The grin dissolved from the girl's face, who remained perfectly still. Tentatively, she asked, "What's wrong?"

"Have a seat. I won't bite."

Voice rising in fear that she'd been caught reading someone else's letter, Sylvia weakly repeated, "What's wrong?"

Ginny dried her hands on a red-and-white striped towel. "Some days are just harder than others. I miss my father. I most certainly miss my mother. It's been so long since she held me in her arms that I'm afraid I am forgetting her. I miss Bill, terribly. And though I see my sisters, they too are gone from this house. Unless I have the radio on or someone comes for tutoring, I don't hear another human voice till I am back at school the next morning."

The girl's shoulders dropped. She tentatively made her way to the kitchen table to sit down. "*I'd* give anything for a little quiet. At home, you can't hear yourself think, and there's nowhere to hide. 'Cause the moment I try, Ma is sure to notice and start screaming about something or other that I didn't do yet."

"Don't be so sure you wouldn't miss them if they weren't around. Silence requires courage not to buckle under the weight of it. I can do it, Sylvia. Silence and I are old acquaintances. I have learned to live by myself, and to manage quite well despite the hard days when they come. But I want you to understand, knowing you has made a difference, has made it easier."

Sylvia, astonished that anyone would think such a thing about her, managed merely to shrug. It took everything she had to keep from grinning.

CHAPTER 12

INNY OPENED THE FRONT DOOR early Saturday morning to find Salvatore standing there, hat in hand, alongside Christina. Once introductions were made, Christina left the two to make their plans. It promised to be a sunny, dry weekend, perfect for outdoor work. Salvatore, having determined what had to be done, even offered to remove from the garage anything that needed to be thrown away to make more room for Ginny's car.

Around noon, when Angela and the boys came by to bring him lunch, an old bicycle and even older tricycle were about to go out onto the curb. Angela had also brought cookies for Miss Ginny, who in turn invited her and the boys to stay for iced tea.

The women sat chatting at the picnic table under the large oak, while the boys grabbed the bikes and began racing up and down the long driveway, chasing each other and occasionally clipping the honeysuckle that clung to the side of the house and made it difficult for a car to navigate the narrow driveway. Angela was about to scold them when Ginny laughed, assuring her no harm had been done.

"The boys are saving me the trouble of trimming back the bush." She placed another one of Angela's sesame cookies on a plate before casually adding, "And if they want to *take* the bicycles, it would please me to see them being put to good use. With a fresh coat of paint, they'll be good as new."

Salvatore, taking a break, wandered over to the women. Ginny handed him an iced tea. Gazing about a garden filled with roses, mint, hydrangea, honeysuckle, and his family, he took a sip of the cold drink and said, "Everything is okay."

The next morning, a knock at the kitchen window alerted Ginny that Sylvia was about to breeze through the freshly painted back door. Ever since their talk, everything she taught her pupil had come together. No longer the skinny girl Ginny had met months before, in an absurd red hat, *this* young woman was a study in poise— dressed in powder blue gingham, including a straw hat pushed forward on her head to shade her face. Everything about her had softened, with pink lipstick replacing the harsh red. Occasional flashes of anger still crossed Sylvia's face, but Ginny noticed they didn't happen as often or last as long.

"You're early today."

"I finished Ma's chores as quick as I could. She didn't believe me when I said I was done." Giggling, she added, "When I showed her, I think it was the first time I'd ever seen her speechless."

Salvatore knocked at the kitchen door and asked if Miss Spencer would come take a look at the ladder. "Look here." He pointed to a rung near the very top of the ladder. "It has a crack in this step. I can use it today, but I don't know how long it is going to last."

Ginny inspected it with some concern. "I don't want you taking any chances. I'll go to the hardware store at once to get you a new one."

"No need to—I can reach the gutters without using this step. I will be careful. I want you to know so no one else gets hurt." He left before she could say another word.

"Who's he?" Sylvia asked.

"That's Mr. Salvatore Samartino. He's finished up some repairs," Ginny explained, gesturing at the kitchen door, "and now he's clearing the gutters. Long overdue. It was a chore my father insisted on doing almost till the very end." She shook her head, thinking about her father paying absolutely no attention to her objections as he climbed the ladder at the age of eighty-four.

"Ready for some iced tea and a discussion of Robert Browning?"

"You bet!"

But it wasn't long after they settled down at the table under the oak tree before Sylvia asked, with a quaver in her voice, "Have you heard from Buddy lately?"

"No, but I assumed you had."

Sylvia shook her head. "I haven't been to church in a long time, but I've stopped by to light a candle and say a prayer for Buddy every day this week." She started to wipe her tears with the palm of her hand, but thinking better of it reached for an embroidered handkerchief in her pocket to dab her eyes. "You won't hurt my feelings if you tell me you *have* heard from him."

"No," Ginny said after a long pause, "I've had nothing for a couple of weeks. But the fighting's been fierce, and, well, no news is good news."

They looked at each other silently, holding back their fears.

Book Three

1998

CHAPTER 13

I SMENE, WHO HAS BEEN PUTTING the finishing touches on her carved pumpkin, grabs a small glass votive filled with a white candle, tucks the matches into her pocket, and opens the front door. She sets the pumpkin down beside the door, lights the candle, and stands back to admire her work. It's a scary pumpkin face—a cross between foo dog and angry beaver. She repositions the hand-made witch's broom she left leaning against the other side of the door. With a smile, she looks up at the huge maple tree, ablaze in glorious reds and oranges, and begins to hum "Maple Leaf Rag." There's a chill in the air; she quickly shuts the door behind her, still humming as she checks on the *brandade* in the oven. She's remembered that Mr. Handelman enjoys an occasional bratwurst and waits for the gratin to finish before cooking the sausage. The beef stew is warming on the stove top.

Halloween is more than two weeks away, but she's decided to celebrate early with a small dinner party to which the guests will come in costume. She is Glinda, the Good Witch. All that luscious pink-and-silver tulle shows her small waist to its best advantage and gives her an excuse to extract Grandmother's coming-out tiara from the bank vault. Her daughter, on the other hand, insists on dressing up as Robin Hood: Dear Lord, a vision in brown and green.

But when Annie comes down to help with the last-minute details, Ismene is pleasantly surprised. The girl's green beret, a hat that once belonged to Ginny, set at jaunty angle, allows her curls to frame her face in a gamine sort of way. And while her daughter's makeup is toned down to make her look convincingly swashbucklerish, she has played up her eyes more than enough to insure a second glance from the opposite sex. The brown tunic is short, and the tights, albeit forest green, show off her legs to advantage.

"Did you take a glance at my apple pie?" Annie asks.

"Yes, lovely."

"And salad?"

"Arugula, persimmons, and pomegranates. Would never have thought of the combination."

Annie looks uncertain.

Shaking her head, Ismene adds, "Don't second guess yourself so much. Be certain the salad is delicious, and it will be." She pats her daughter's cheek and continues, as she hands her small plates, "Successful entertaining requires planning, but it also needs confidence." Seeing Annie finally return her smile, Ismene launches into her list of instructions. "Take everything on the kitchen table and put it on the coffee table. Then fill seven goody bags with two of each kind of chocolate from the Little Shop. There's orange-and- black ribbon for you to tie them off. When you're finished, they go to the left of every place setting in the dining room. And,

Annie, absolutely *no* sampling of the candy before dinner, do you hear me?"

THE GUESTS HAVE SETTLED IN THE PARLOR: Margie as a '20s flapper, Jim in a tux as 007, Andrew as a pirate, Christina Hill as a black cat with Alma purring on her lap, and Rudy Handelman, as a tin soldier, has just popped the champagne cork when the doorbell rings. Ismene puts the sausage slices on the coffee table, then goes to open the door.

For a moment, she simply stares at the person facing her, then shrieks and runs up the stairs.

Annie races to the front door with Andrew right behind her to see a rather mild-mannered, bony man in a beautiful gray sweater and black jeans, sporting a long, graying ponytail.

"Ah, Annie? You *are* Annie, aren't you? You look like your mother."

"Yes? Can I help you?"

"Ah, well, yes. You've turned out rather nicely, by the way. Very pretty." He looks up at the maple tree as if asking it for some help.

"This is a bit awkward." He sighs, shaking his head. "Damn it. Of course it's *very* awkward." Almost speaking to himself, he continues, "Clearly, there is no easy way to say it. Stupid of me to think that there *would* be."

He squares his shoulders and releases a long breath. "Well, stupid or not, here I am. . .Annie, I'm your father—Gabriel, Gabriel Clairmont."

Ismene, now completely composed, has slowly descended the stairs and takes charge. "Andrew, be a dear and bring another champagne glass from the kitchen."

"No, thank you, Ismene, but no. I don't drink alcohol anymore."

Barely able to contain herself, Ismene asks, "Does that mean that you've finally Found Yourself?"

"...Ah, yes, you could say that I have. Yes, indeed."

"How far did you have to look?" she snaps.

"Oh, well, I've been all over. Brazil, Argentina, Baha, Egypt, Ivory Coast...oh, yes and British Columbia and Alaska for a while. Spent some time in Majorca, Sardinia, southern France. Finally, I drifted to the Netherlands. I—I live in Rotterdam now." He looks down at his feet, clears his throat. "Ismene, I've come a long way. Please, may I come in?"

"I don't know, Gabriel—this is not my home, it's our daughter's. You'll have to ask her."

Annie, white as a sheet, nods silently and allows him to pass through. Jim and Margie open a space between them on the couch to make room for her to sit. Jim places a protective arm around his cousin's shoulder. Margie grabs Annie's freezing hands and whispers, "This is news to us!"

Rudy Handelman has risen to make excuses for himself and his nephew when Ismene raises her hand to silence the confused man. "I insist you all stay. Please."

Andrew, with no intention of budging from the room regardless of what his uncle thinks is appropriate, pulls a dining room chair into the parlor for the unexpected guest and studies him, cross-armed, from behind Ismene's customary wingback chair. Christina Hill, who has guessed more of this story than she's let on, quietly sips her champagne, ready to help if needed. She pets the cat, now on the alert that something in the room has shifted.

Ismene begins the introductions. "My niece and nephew, Jim and Margie Singleton. This is Mr. Rudolph Handelman, who lives across the street, and his nephew Andrew Rourke. Mrs. Christina Hill—whom you met at our wedding but doubtless don't remember—lives three houses up the street. Everyone, this is my dead husband Gabriel."

Annie finally finds her voice. "I don't understand."

"Yes, I know," he replies as his wife hands him a glass of fresh cider. Aware of seven pairs of eyes looking at him, he accepts it. "You see," he goes on but stops, thinking about how he used to be. "I didn't like who I had become. I drank a lot and chased women a lot. And needed time to straighten myself out. So I dropped off the face of the Earth," he tells Annie. "I set up the trust that would keep you and your mother comfortable for the rest of your lives. The lawyers have taken care of the payments all these years. Our agreement—your mother's and mine—was that I was to be dead to the world, and that she mustn't try to find me until I returned. And I must say, Ismene, you kept your side of the bargain beautifully."

She responds with a regal nod.

"I suppose it was a cowardly thing to do," he goes on uneasily, "but I was desperate, and I believed in my heart that, if I continued as I was, I'd be dead for real soon enough."

He notices Ismene wince. "I'm sorry, Ismene—so very, very sorry." He swallows some cider and again searches Annie's gaze. "First, I had to deal with the booze. I needed to do something that would take my mind off it. By happenstance, a fluke really, I got hired as a short order cook in British Columbia. It was hard work and long hours, which kept me out of trouble. But it didn't take long for me to realize I had a knack for cooking. And I discovered I enjoyed feeding people. I began traveling from restaurant to restaurant, wherever they'd take me, learning what I could, eventually working my way up to chef. Learning to be creative with food kept my hands busy and my heart full. And I realized with a start one day that I'd found my own way to stop drinking...and a reason not to chase after women, too."

Again Ismene winces, but this time no one notices except Christina, who continues to pet the uneasy cat now wondering whether anyone is going to sneak her some sausage.

"Of course, you don't see," Gabriel goes on, glancing again at Annie. "But...but understand that, all my life, I'd been eager to prove to myself, and everybody else, that I was something I wasn't. But no matter how many women I bedded—" he shrugs and meets Ismene's icy stare— "no matter how many times I hurt you, Ismene, then confessed my misdeeds, promised not to do them again, then did them again...it never changed who I was. Am." Taking a deep breath, he continues, "The Dutch have passed legislation allowing for same-sex partnerships to be recognized under the law, and parliament has also resolved to tackle the issue of gay marriage as a legal right in the near future...and so, ah, Roger has asked me to make an honest man of him."

He stops to look around the room; no one moves or makes a sound. "The financial arrangements for you and Annie will continue," he adds after a long pause. "We, Roger and I, have a rather successful restaurant in Rotterdam.... So—so I'm here, Ismene, at long a last to ask you for a divorce."

Ismene smiles, for the first time showing any sign of softening toward him. "I'm glad you found your way, Gabriel, really. I. . .for years I've tortured myself, wondering where I failed us." She looks away for some time before facing her husband once more. "Now I can begin to understand. . .and begin to forgive you. And forgive me, too. " She breaks into laughter and, catching her breath, adds, "And I will be *delighted* to divorce you."

He begins to laugh in relief. Soon enough, they rise to give each other a hug.

Annie refrains from asking the question that no one seems to think is important: *What about me?*

Ismene has soon asked Gabriel to stay for dinner—and without knowing exactly how it happened, the guests divide up with the men discussing Dutch politics on one end of the room, and the women, in a close knot at the other end, murmuring among themselves until they eventually clear the remains of the food from the coffee table. In the kitchen, Ismene focuses on getting dinner to the dining room.

Annie, meanwhile, ignoring the bustle around her, looks out the kitchen window to find the red fox sitting with her kits, nearly fully grown, by the holly bush. The girl looks down when Alma complains about being fed. She focuses on cutting into tiny pieces enough left-over sausage to fill the cat dish. Alma meows her thanks before digging in. Annie squats to pet her and surreptitiously wipes away the tears starting to form at the corner of her eyes.

When she hears Margie clear her throat, she looks up, and her cousin says, "I know you've got other things on your mind right now. But I asked my mother about the photo you gave me." She hands the picture back to Annie. "Mom had no idea, but she suggested asking

Granny Grace to take a look at it. The girl is Sylvia Ahearn—"

"I know," Annie interrupts. "That *femme fatale* at Le Mangoire is her granddaughter."

"Yeah, yeah, but let me finish," Margie goes on, swiping her bangs to one side. "Sylvia came from the other side of town, but somehow she got close to Aunt Ginny. It supposedly started out as a sort of a pupil-teacher thing, where she helped Sylvia learn to behave more like a lady. And the *guy* in the photo is Buddy Crocker, someone Aunt Ginny's fiancé, Bill, was friends with during the war. According to Granny Grace, Aunt Ginny was a bit keen on him, too, though she vehemently denied it when Granny teased her about it. Aunt Ginny was all *for* those two getting married here in this house."

Giving her cousin a hand to get up from the floor, Margie continues, "One question I have that *I'd* like answered is—*did* the wedding take place here? In all the stories we've heard over the years from Aunt Ginny and Granny Grace, no one has ever mentioned a wedding under this roof."

"Margie—" Ismene is smiling sweetly—"could you tear yourself away from Annie long enough to take the salad and the potatoes out onto the table in the dining room?

"Annie, have you filled the water glasses yet? And fill your father's wine glass with more cider.

"Christina, would you be a dear and put the bread basket on the table? Thank you all so much. I believe dinner is ready."

Once everyone is seated, Annie finds herself next to her father— an absolute stranger. Although it's been more than twenty years since the last time she remembers him being in her life, and during that time she's longed more than once for the chance to talk to him, she can't think of a thing to say besides, "What about me?"

It seems as if he has read her mind. He lays his fork down, dabs his mouth with the linen napkin. "I know this is really difficult for you to comprehend. But I hope you eventually come to see that, sometimes, what seems harsh and callous is really an unselfish act of love, improbable as it seems."

He collects his thoughts for a moment before continuing. "My, uh, my father was a drunk with a bad temper and a heavy hand." His face clouds over for a moment. "Then. . .then divorce wasn't so easy as it is now. Though it did happen. But looking back on those years, I'm not sure that my mother would have had the backbone to go it alone.

"And. . .and that's what I love so much about your mother. She's strong-willed." He smiles as he glances at Ismene, who smiles back before answering Rudy's question about the still life over the credenza, which has replaced the hunting scene that hung in that spot for as long as he can remember.

"With me drinking more and more, Annie, I was afraid, and so was she, that I'd turn into my father. I wouldn't chance that for anything. I loved you then, and I still do. So does your mother. She would have killed me before allowing any harm to come to you. That's why you spent so much time here in this house as a very little girl, to be. . .safe while I sobered up long enough to get drunk again."

". . .But if I understand correctly, you've been sober for a while. Why *now*—why not last year, or two years ago? Didn't you want me in your life?"

"Annie, after so many years. . .each time I thought about getting in touch with you, I lost my nerve. I've never had your mother's certainties about *anything* in life. I can only hope you come to see that you mattered enough to me to make myself scarce rather than have you carry the kind of memories I do of *my* father."

He again looks away for a while, trying to find a coherent means of explaining the unexplainable to his daughter. "Finally, finally. . .after falling in love with Roger, having the courage to stay in a relationship and *not* become my biggest fear, that's pushed me to risk rejection from you. To knock on your door, hat in hand, and take a stab at fatherhood, belated as it is."

It is her turn to consider what to say next. "Roger. . .your fiancé, he seems special."

"Yes, he is. But so are you." A mischievous look crosses his face. "Of *that*, I'm certain. Takes a person of great integrity to share a house with Ismene."

Annie giggles. It seems she has an ally in the Ismene wars, even if a rather distant one.

CHAPTER 14

JOEY SAMARTINO IS SITTING at the same yellow Formica table in his mother's kitchen that the whole family sat at nearly half a century ago. Nothing much has changed except a few added coats of paint to the cabinets, which remain white, and the walls, which remain buttercup yellow. But it's been a long time since he and his brother chased each other around the table. Everything, and everyone, in the room is a little worse for the wear.

He watches his mother take out a cookie sheet filled with sesame cookies. Even as a child, he could never wait for those cookies to cool, and he reaches for one. His mother slaps his hand. "Five minutes."

"But—"

"Five minutes!"

He has occupied her dead husband's chair, a tip-off to her that he's here in the middle of the afternoon, on a weekday, for a reason. Silently, she refills his coffee cup, takes a seat facing him—the same way she faced her husband whenever something was eating him—

and waits.

Joey shifts in his seat to face her. "Ma, it's the first time in a long time that someone's planning to run against me from my own party. I gotta confess, I don't like it."

"Oh?"

"Yeah—I mean, I've done my best for. . .for everyone, not just those who vote for me. . .and it seems as if it's not enough."

"Do you *want* to be mayor again?"

"Honestly? . . . I don't know if I want to run for reelection next year."

"Yes or no? Simple enough."

"Nothing is very simple in politics these days. Now you run for election, win, get sworn in the second of January, and the next day you're running again. No one works together anymore."

She gives him a sad smile. "One day, sooner or later, you will be replaced. Either you lose an election or you die, but someone will eventually replace you."

"Ah, come on."

"No, Joey, no *come on*. Listen to an old woman who can no longer ignore the inevitable." She gets up, pours herself a cup of coffee to warm her hands, and gives him a plate of cookies. "I am trying to say I love you and I am proud of you, but everyone is replaceable in the end. The tapestry of life is that one thread finishes and another picks up where the first ends. The rhythm of life never changes."

"How is being depressed that I'll eventually be reduced to a photo hanging in the borough hall supposed to help me decide whether or not to run?"

"Maybe this is the time for you to decide what you want to pass on to the next generation—what you've *learned*. Hm?" She sips some hot coffee. "Neither of your children care for politics. But *this* young man is hungry." She studies her son scowling for a moment before continuing, "Run, Joey, or don't run, but let your political legacy be for the *living. . .about* living."

They sit in silence for some time before he grudgingly admits, "Well, I'll give you that none of us up on the dais is getting any younger." He takes a bite of a cookie and looks out the window.

"There are many ways to teach honor. In politics, it's how to run for an election. How to win, and how to lose. How to play the political game so that you can sleep at night. My son, what will you choose to *teach? That* is your true legacy, not a photo hanging in a hallway."

He says nothing for a while, finishing his coffee and plate of cookies before taking his leave. As he gives her a kiss on the cheek, he says, "Okay, Mom, I hear you, but no promises. Turning the other cheek with this little snot isn't so easy. But I will give what you say some thought."

He decides to play hooky from work that afternoon and heads home, thinking that he doesn't like any of the choices his mother has laid out for him, so it's with a welcome relief that he hears Paul Demaria call out his name from his kitchen door.

"Hey, Joey, I got some information for you about the. . .you know." He drops his voice to a whisper. ". . .about the Ahearns. Better come in for a cup of coffee, so we can talk private."

Joey makes his way up the stairs and through the side door, which leads straight into the kitchen. Although he has already had two cups, he accepts the mug that Paul offers him with a nod and asks, "What gives?"

They sit down at the red Formica table. "I been asking around all quiet-like about the family. Harriet Ahearn's husband, Tom Greene, skipped out long ago with a younger and prettier woman. He never stopped running till he got to California. And he's never been back."

Joey shrugs. "Bad marriages come a dime a dozen. Not everyone is as lucky as we are." He sips some coffee to be polite. "And I wouldn't want to tempt fate by throwing the first stone." He smiles, thinking about his mother's advice.

"Yeah, but there's more. One of the other sisters, Sylvia, maybe wasn't so lucky either. There's talk that she was in the family way, long ago, when it wasn't so common as it is now. But she didn't get married around here. In fact, she disappeared. And the family's never mentioned her. Not until lately anyway."

Joey sucks on a tooth. "What's changed?"

"Her granddaughter's come here for a visit." Paul raises his index finger. "*And* she been seen around town with *Robert Greene*. Harriet's been clucking up a storm about the two of them."

". . .So what have we got on our hands at best, Paul, a couple of kissing cousins?"

"Joey, there ain't no such thing as *coincidences*." Paul jumps up from the table and paces from the sink to the refrigerator and back in his excitement. "There's gotta be some reason for the bad blood between the Spencers and Ahearns. And you know, it don't take much to get on the wrong side of *that* clan."

He seats himself back at the table, hands waving as he continues, "My sister-in-law, Jeannie, was in the same class as Sylvia, and they used to be pals. Until, that is, Sylvia got chummy with Ginny. Then Sylvia became too *fine* for any of her old friends. Jeannie tells me Sylvia got engaged and was planning a wedding, but suddenly the wedding didn't happen and she went off to live in Oklahoma. Nobody's," he points out, "heard about her actually getting married, not even Christina Hill, who knows everything. Believe me, I checked around."

Joey sighs. "Paul, why should either you or I give a damn about any of this?"

"You said yourself that Ginny Spencer was loved by all, so this attack don't make sense. But Ginny's not dead three months, and there's all kind of talk about her and the skull goin' around town. Harriet and her family have been talking a lot of trash. Maybe it's to get at you and help her son, but *maybe* it's to get back at Ginny. Or maybe a little bit of both."

ROBERT GREENE STRAIGHTENS HIS BOW TIE and flings the black cape, lined in crimson, around his shoulders. He stands back to admire himself in the full-length mirror, trying to decide whether or not to wear the fangs he bought. Dressed for a Halloween party, he is in no particular hurry to get there. He wants to be sure he'll be fashionably late. Making an entrance with Lara on his arm will certainly turn a few heads in his direction. She is going as Lillian Gish, wild-eyed and wild-haired, playing a beautiful damsel in distress to his Dracula. How delicious.

As he again adjusts the cape, shifting it forward to admire the full sweep of the folds cascading in front, he asks himself if it would be a good thing for him to be in love with Lara. She's not the rich wife he imagines he'll eventually find for himself to help finance his career in politics. But she's gorgeous, built, knows how to move that body of hers to its fullest effect, even knows when to talk and when to keep her mouth shut. What more could he possibly want in a wife, except a lot of money?

And if he is honest with himself, it's obvious she is very attracted to him. Maybe even a little bit in love with him already. She hangs on his every word. Never misses a chance to give him her little special pout that spreads into a come-hither smile. Well, why should it be so surprising; after all, meeting an attractive up-and-coming lawyer from the East coast must be. . .must be overwhelming, if he's been reading her signals right.

He decides to leave the fangs at home. If the moment is right, when he makes his move, he doesn't want to be pulling plastic out of his mouth.

BOB AHEARN HATES COSTUME PARTIES, but his wife Elaine has insisted that a Halloween party will be a fun way to repay those to whom they have social obligations. He scowls at the mirror as he slaps on his coonskin cap and yanks up his powder blue britches. He's going as Benjamin Franklin. He settles the wire-rimmed glasses on the tip of his nose and reminds himself that Franklin, too, played the fool to get what *he* wanted—French financial backing of the rebellion. Bob is less sure of what *this* charade will achieve, other than keep his wife happy. He tugs at his collar. Elaine has knotted the lace-edged jabot too tight around his neck, and his silver vest is about ready to pop. He definitely needs a bourbon.

As he makes his way down the staircase, catching a whiff of the mulled cider perfuming the house, the bell chimes, and he opens the front door to be greeted by shouts of trick-or-treat. Guests pile into the hallway with delighted shrieks, guessing each other's costumes. Smiling, he shakes everyone's hand and exchanges enough pleasantries not to appear rude as he points them in the direction of the bartender, who already has his hands full.

The bell rings once more, and he opens the door to find his sister Harriet, nephew Robert, and grandniece Lara all appropriately dressed: Harriet as a witch wearing a pointed black hat, Robert as a vampire fiddling with his cape, and Lara, eyes rimmed in black, blonde hair a mass of banana curls swept to the back—picture-perfect as a silent screen heroine. Now he really needs that bourbon.

"Hello, Harriet." He dutifully kisses his older sister as his shoulders and the upper third of his sternum barely meet hers in an approximate hug. "Don't you look nice."

"Oh, come off it, Bobby." Harriet scowls as she hands him her coat. "Don't bullshit me. What on Earth got into your head to do something as ridiculous as a costume party?"

"*Why?* Don't you think costume parties are fun? Elaine does."

He shakes his nephew's outstretched hand. "How goes it?"

"Doing well, sir." The young man chuckles. "And the skull found on the Spencer roof hasn't hurt us none either."

Bob slaps his nephew's back with a reciprocal chuckle, then leans forward to whisper into his ear, "Let me give you some unsolicited advice. Don't push it."

"But—"

"No." Bob lowers his voice even more to emphasize his point. "If you're smart, you won't use it. Digging up someone else's dirt is an invitation to have yours dug up, too. No one is without regrets, without skeletons, literally or figuratively, somewhere in the attic—"

"If I may say so, Bobby, you're acting like a drip." Harriet then gives her brother one of her wicked laughs. "It certainly would do my heart good to see the Spencers, for once, taken down a peg or two. I would think you of all people would be pleased."

"Revenge has a way of boomeranging at you, Har. As for my being pleased with the character assassination of a dead woman who has no voice to defend herself, I am not. I learned a painful but crucial lesson from Miss Spencer—the sanity-saving importance of being upright. A good thing, don't you think, for a superior court judge to have picked up?"

In no mood, however, to revisit the minutiae of his childhood humiliation with his more than eager sister, he returns his attention to his nephew. "It would be best to keep it to issues that the good townspeople are griping about. Taxes, too much congestion, not enough expert input putting together an updated master plan. But now that Samartino's got you right where he wants you—on the Planning Board— you can be considered as much a part of the problem as anyone else."

He turns his attention at last to the young woman, who has been keenly attentive to this exchange. "Lara." He takes her hand and kisses it. "You are far too beautiful to be subjected to all this boring shop talk. Why don't you take Robert in hand, get something to drink, and have a good time."

Lara flashes him a knowing smile in response and throws her arm around his neck, pressing her body uncomfortably close to his in order to give him a kiss on the cheek. She then grabs Robert's elbow, steering him away from the bar and into the thick of the crowd. As Bob watches the two wander off, he thinks, Poor bastard, he's out of his league.

BOROUGH CLERK JOHN KELLY, MASQUERADING AS HIMSELF in a tux, reaches for a smoked salmon canapé being offered on a silver tray by the clown waiter while Elaine, decked out as an angel, and Douglas Newman, the town coroner cum elf, are kicking around ideas about how to raise money for the library and whom to target for the infusion of additional funds, when he sees Robert T. Greene approach. He is reminded of the family connection when Greene addresses the hostess as Aunt Elaine as he makes the necessary introductions to those standing with her.

"You remember Lara Snow, Aunt Sylvia's granddaughter, from Oklahoma?"

"Hard to forget such a stunning creature." Elaine wraps her arms around the girl and gives her a squeeze. "*So* pleased that you could come, my dear. I must make sure that you meet some of the more eligible bachelors here tonight."

"Well, good looks certainly run in the family," jokes Robert, though he's flushed. Ambivalence dissolved, he vows to make her his sooner than later. Feeling the need to position himself ahead of any possible competition, he gives Lara a wink and asks John, "So how does the prospect of working for a different mayor appeal to you?"

The borough clerk gives Robert a polite smile. "Never a problem. I've worked with different administrations my entire career."

Not quite satisfied with the older man's response, Robert steps forward and squarely faces him to press for a more definitive answer. "Surely you see the need for change? Fresh blood, new ideas?"

To defuse the situation, John shifts his weight to only present the boy his flank before answering, "As Dr. Johnson put it, 'the pleasures of sudden wonder are soon exhausted, and the mind can only repose on the stability of truth.'"

Unsure of what to make of that, Robert tries to turn it to his advantage, heedless of his uncle's advice. "That's my point—truth. Why has no one bothered to find and arrest the person responsible for that skull? Isn't that *also* coming to terms with the truth?"

Lara grabs Robert's arm and draws herself close enough to murmur, "Would you be a darling and get me a drink?"

Electrified by the very musky scent of her perfume, he doesn't have time to be annoyed by the interruption and hurries off at once.

Lara giggles, "What exactly happens now—in search of truth with this terribly mysterious skull found on a roof?"

The coroner has sensed Kelly's growing impatience and steps in. "Since human remains have been found, the skull is being examined by the state medical examiner. They run tests to help the police determine what exactly happened."

Surprised, Lara asks, "Can you find out who the person was?"

Douglas hands his empty glass to a waitress dressed as a nurse and accepts another champagne. "They will certainly try to piece together any clues they uncover."

"What happens if they do find out?"

"Who the person is?" Douglas stokes his beard as he ponders the question. "Well, the family, if they can be found, is notified. But first the investigation has to determine whether the skull is a historical artifact or the result of a recent crime."

There is an awkward lull as everyone considers the specter of death. Lara absentmindedly accepts the wine glass that Robert hands her. "Maybe they'll never find out—and the Spencers will never ever be able to live it down." She smirks at the thought and, once again grabbing Robert by the elbow before he can comment, steers him to the next knot of guests.

John and Douglas exchange glances as the couple depart but say nothing more about the matter. To reduce any awkwardness with their hostess, who seems at a loss for words, Douglas instead pays Elaine a compliment on her choice of champagne, then turns the conversation back to library funding.

CHAPTER 15

ARLY IN THE EVENING A FEW DAYS LATER, Jack Martin whistles softly after Andrew has described the Clairmont Halloween party. They are sitting at the farthest booth in the back room at CJ's for privacy, under dimmed lights, each nursing a beer.

"Oh, boy," Jack laughs, shaking his head. "She's a firecracker, that one. *Never* a dull moment."

"Mm, yeah."

"So what did she say when her resurrected dad suddenly appeared at the door?"

Andrew shrugs. "What can you say, really? She went white from shock. But to her credit, she allowed him the courtesy to tell his story, and then took it like a trouper. That's my point, she's different."

"Different is an understatement." Jack ticks off the list with his fingers. "First you find a human skull on her roof. Then after twenty years, her dead father shows up to announce he's no longer a drunk but *is* now gay, wants to marry Roger, divorce her mother, and—as a result—is invited to stay for dinner!"

"You're missing the point, Jack."

"Oh? What's that?"

"Most people would have been leery about the skull. Instead, she goes to reach for it and then wraps it up to keep it safe. At dinner, I watched her from the other end of the table as she spoke with her father—they were laughing together. I'm telling you, she's. . .different."

"Okay, man, I get that. But, you know—" Jack waves a finger in the air for emphasis before finishing his thought— "different can get to be a challenge after a while."

". . .You could be right." Andrew considers the point as he rubs his face. "But what strikes me about her, no matter what crazy thing is happening at any given moment, is. . .is that she's *kind*. Not fake kind—manners meant not to rock the boat in social situations—but truly kind at heart. *That's* so rare these days."

Laying on a thick Irish brogue, Jack replies. "Ah, me boy, you must be smitten. To be sure, findin' yourself a silver lining in a matter any sensible body would consider doubtful means Cupid's arrow has pierced yer heart. Bless your trustin' soul."

"Very funny. I'm not saying any of this makes sense. But who else can I talk to, if not you?"

"Well, if you are serious about *considering* getting serious, once the matter of the skull and *The Secret of the 99 Steps* has officially been cleared, Rachel and I could invite you and Nancy Drew over for dinner one night. My wife's got the best shit detector I've ever seen."

"Since when did you read Nancy Drew books?"

"Got a sister, remember?"

"Yeah, but you know the *titles?*"

"Shut up." Jack drops a couple of bills on the table as he grabs his jacket and keys to head home to his pregnant wife. "My treat. Good to catch up." He smiles and adds, "And good to see you happy."

Andrew finishes his beer and decides to order some food. He has started to hail the waitress coming toward him when he realizes it's Annie. He immediately gets up and stammers, "Hi! Um, what brings you here?"

"Well, your uncle said this is one of your haunts. I happened to be driving by, saw your truck in the lot, and was hoping to ask you, face to face, for a favor. When I bumped into your policeman friend at the door, he told me that you were here in the back room."

"*Did* he!—I mean, he *did?* That's thoughtful of him." He gestures toward the booth. "Please, won't you sit down?"

She removes her gray scarf and burgundy jacket, and takes a seat. Within seconds, the waitress appears. Andrew convinces Annie to join him for a burger and fries along with a beer.

Once the waitress leaves with their order, Annie gets right to the point. "I want to ask your help in a matter that doesn't concern you, but you're the only person I know who knows practically everybody in town. I've promised myself to get to the bottom of this skull mess—no matter what the outcome is. Anything will be better than living under a shadow of foul play."

Andrew considers this for a moment. "If I can help, sure. What do you think I can do?"

She gives him a searching look. "You're not just being polite."

"Believe me, I'm pretty good at saying no if I want to."

It's Annie's turn to consider her reply. "Well, first I want to put on the table what I *know* and what I *suspect*. I visited Aunt Ginny from the time I was a toddler. I can't recall anyone who was ever cross with her—except maybe my mother, just a little, and that's probably my fault for making her feel second-best when it came to my affection.

"I've spent a lot of time in the attic and in Aunt Ginny's bedroom, looking for anything that could shed some light on the skull. So far there's nothing out of the ordinary, and, thank God, no other skeletal remains to be found anywhere. There *is* one photo I found in the attic in which, initially, I couldn't place who the people were. They weren't meticulously identified, like the rest. And that one's connected to a couple of coincidences that may or may not have something to do with the skull."

She reaches into her handbag and hands the image to him.

"It was taken in the '40s. I now know that the other woman with her arm around Aunt Ginny's waist is Robert Greene's aunt and Lara Snow's grandmother, Sylvia Ahearn. The man standing with them is Buddy Crocker. He is Lara's grandfather. I showed this picture to your uncle last night. All he said was that he remembers Sylvia Ahearn was a pupil of Aunt Ginny's for a while. Then Sylvia stopped coming around."

Their burgers arrive, and for a few minutes they eat in silence.

"So. . .you think my uncle is holding out?" he says before taking a sip of his beer.

"I think your uncle is too much of a gentleman to gossip, especially when he's not sure he's gotten the story right."

Andrew nods in agreement.

"Normally," she continues, "I'd simply chalk up Robert Greene's interest in the skull to political shenanigans, except that, around the same time as you discovered the skull, Lara Snow knocked at my door and insinuated herself enough into my mother's good graces for me to find the two of them in the parlor, drinking coffee. But my mother remained polite almost to a fault, which tipped me off that she wasn't happy about our guest.

"Lara eventually asked me to show her the house, and as we walked around, she muttered a strange phrase—'not hers, not hers at all.' I remember this unnerved me enough to steer the tour into the garden, where it was easier to say good-bye and end the visit. Yet my mother refuses to discuss the incident." Annie throws up her hands. "Picture *my mother* refraining from voicing her opinion about anything!"

Andrew chews on another fry and thinks about this for a while. "I hate to say it, but this seems like a whole lot of nothing amounting to not much."

"Look, maybe the point of Lara's visit *was* to spy on our family for Greene, but it felt more personal than that. She kept emphasizing the close relationship between her grandmother and my great-aunt, and how much Aunt Ginny admired her. Over the years, I heard lots of stories about Aunt Ginny's students. But here's the thing—I never *once* heard my great-aunt talk about Sylvia Ahearn. Assuming Lara was telling the truth, why not? And since I'm listing unanswered questions, I'll throw in one my *mother* has raised a couple of times— why didn't Aunt Ginny ever get married?"

Andrew quietly replies, "Sometimes the right person never

comes along." His doubts persist, but he clears his throat to ask, "You really think any of this is connected?"

"Could be. Our grandmother, Aunt Ginny's sister, took a look at this photo, and it jogged her memory enough to say there'd been talk of Sylvia Ahearn getting married at our home. But as far as anyone can tell, she didn't. Maybe she simply decided to get married somewhere else. Nobody seems to know *what* happened."

"...You want me to ask my uncle about all this."

"Even if he doesn't know about the wedding, ask him if he remembers when Sylvia Ahearn spent time with Aunt Ginny. At least it would narrow my search at the library to when the Ahearn engagement was announced, or where the marriage took place."

Andrew shakes his head. "It still seems to me like a lot of effort for a long shot at best."

"I know. But I haven't got another lead to follow."

"...I see your point. Okay, I'll do my best to get my uncle to talk."

Annie looks unconvinced.

"I promise," he insists. "I will look into this. But to change the subject—how are you getting on with your dad and mom these days?"

She leans forward on her elbows. "Well, my dad left yesterday. But while he was here, you'd have thought the prospect of divorce would make things difficult. Instead, I watched my parents chat together like old friends, swapping recipes, even cooking together. My mother's like a different human being."

Andrew laughs. "Your mother is *always* a little different."

"Believe me, I know." Annie's smile doesn't fade as she continues,

"She's happier than I've ever seen her. As if a tremendous burden has been lifted from her shoulders. I guess carrying that kind of a secret was hard."

Andrew reaches across the table to pat her hand. "It still must be a real shock for you—"

"To realize just how many family secrets we have? You bet! I'm still coming to terms with what my parents have told me *since* the dinner party. Neither wanted to admit they had a failing relationship. They decided on a second honeymoon in the Levant and left me in Aunt Ginny's care. It very soon became obvious that, no matter how romantic the setting, the marriage was over. Sickened with grief and not thinking, my mother agreed to my father's plan, hoping that, if she gave him what he wanted, he'd come back to her in the end, and they'd figure out some way to make it work.

"Since my father has no living relatives, and my mother's family was painfully aware of the problems she'd endured, the story of his death in Istanbul was accepted. The lawyers had always been in charge of managing the trust fund, so my mother soldiered on. But when his absence dragged on from months to years, she began to believe that the story she'd been asked to tell eventually came true."

She takes a bite of her hamburger, chews, and swallows before continuing, "As for getting on with my father, I must say I can see why my mother fell for him. He's a lovely man, but he's also a stranger."

"Can't be easy to bridge so many years of absence."

"No, but this situation is forcing me to become patient and allow the relationship to unfold with time." She bites her lip and adds, "It's weird. Once my father legalizes his relationship with Roger in Holland, I will have gone from having no father to having two in a matter of months."

Andrew's curiosity gets the better of him. "Are you going to visit them anytime soon?"

"Are you kidding? Before he left yesterday to return home, I was invited to visit him and Roger soon, even attend the wedding when it takes place. My mother accepted my dad's invitation on the behalf of both of us. She's determined we are to be one happy albeit atypical family."

Andrew picks up his beer. "I say cheers to that."

Annie giggles, raising her glass to meet his. "In for a penny, in for a pound."

MARGIE ROLLS HER EYES as she strolls toward the borough hall with Annie for the Mayor and Council meeting that will shortly begin. Annie has decided that, rather than read about her home in the newspaper the following day, she will listen first-hand to what is being bandied about, should the subject of the skull come up again. Margie has agreed to keep her company.

"You're unbelievable," Margie groans. "How can you say it wasn't a date? Of *course* it was a date. Didn't he pay for the meal?"

"Well, yes. But—"

"But *nothing!* If I were in your place and he bought me a cup of *coffee*, I'd say it was a date. He's smart, good-looking, really likeable, and *clearly* interested in *you.*"

"What are you talking about? It's not as if he asked me out for dinner. I showed up while he was about to order some food, and—"

"He asked you to join him."

"...Yes, he did ask me to join him." Annie tugs her jacket down in annoyance. "Honestly, Margie, if I thought for one moment that he was going to pay for my meal, I'd have said no. He simply refused to split the bill when the check came."

"So it *was* a date. And not only did he pay, he said he'd help you find out more about the picture, right?"

Annie's jaw tightens. "Yes."

"So he's willing to dig around into Aunt Ginny's life, essentially a complete stranger, because he's got nothing better to do? Or is it, maybe, because he likes you enough to be willing to help out?"

"All right!" Annie concedes the one point regarding the date in order to halt further discussion about the other. "You could say it was a date by default. But Margie, for someone who insists she's a pragmatist, you're really a hopeless romantic at heart."

Margie gives her cousin a wink. "Yep. But if you dare tell anyone, I will deny it."

They are surprised to find the meeting room crowded. They slip into two unoccupied seats in the back. When Margie sees no one she knows in the audience, she gets up to inspect the black-and-white portraits of long-dead mayors from the late-nineteenth and twentieth centuries that surround the room. The sun has set, and the yellow glow of the overhead lights reflected in the window panes has obliterated the view of the grounds outside. At the dais up front, the last to take his seat is the borough clerk, John Kelly, while the others settle into expectant stillness. Mayor Samartino adjusts the mike in front of him and bangs the gavel, bringing the meeting to order.

The council is considering introducing an ordinance restricting parking. The law would prevent anyone without a town sticker from parking more than two hours on streets between 8:00 a.m. and noon, Monday through Friday.

When the meeting is opened to the public for comments or questions regarding the proposal, an elderly gentleman, ramrod straight in a blue blazer, a pink shirt, and red plaid pants, approaches the mike with the aid of a carved walnut cane. Theodore Blauvelt introduces himself, giving his address for the public record, since all public meetings are recorded, and begins to voice his objections. "Why should the town have to take on this expense—a waste of money printing up and distributing decals?"

Eddie Polansky, with a fresh crew cut and shave, who pushed the ordinance for consideration, adjusts his thick black glasses and clears his throat. "We have commuters from out of town parking here to grab a bus headed for New York. It's cheaper and faster than wherever they're coming from. As a result, there are fewer available parking spaces for residents. This ordinance is an attempt to free up parking for people who live here."

"Maybe so, though no one has offered any concrete evidence to support this, but I don't appreciate the bother of having to come to town hall to obtain stickers for my car and my wife's."

"Mr. Blauvelt, you would only have to do this once every three years. But if, for some reason, you don't wish to obtain a residential sticker and can manage to keep your cars or any guest's car in your driveway during those times, then a sticker won't be necessary."

"Young man," Mr. Blauvelt, who has drawn himself even more erect in order to expand his chest at what he considers an impertinence, rumbles on, "I have lived here all my life, as have my parents and grandparents, and there's never been an issue until now."

"I've lived here all my life, too, Mr. Blauvelt," replies Eddie. "I remember as a kid when, just a few miles north of us, it was all dense woods. I'd take my bike up there to explore to my heart's content. But a good deal of that is built up now. This ordinance will prohibit outsiders from using our streets as a free park-and-ride to get to work."

"What about customers? This is terrible for businesses," shouts a Korean woman, sitting on the edge of her chair in the front row. She owns a bakery on Main Street, and a number of other business owners from the same vicinity, surrounding her, grumble in agreement.

Mr. Blauvelt cedes the mike her.

"My customers will go elsewhere."

"The law will allow *anyone* to park on our street weekdays mornings for up to two hours. I know your bakery very well, Mrs. Park. A bit too well." Eddie pats his protruding tummy and gets a laugh from the audience. "I've stood on lines long enough to wonder, when I get to the counter, if I'll be able to buy some of your famous cream puffs. Even so, I've never had to wait one hour, let alone two, to buy anything from you. Your shop is as efficient as your desserts are delicious."

The woman, preening in spite of herself at the endorsement of her business acumen as well as her cream puffs, simply follows up with a question about guest parking, should a driveway not be available.

"If you anticipate having a visitor, or even a customer, exceeding the two-hour limit on weekdays, guest permits will be available upon request."

Margie whispers, "This is better than TV."

Annie shushes her as Robert Greene ambles to the mike, making sure every pair of eyes in the room is following him.

"Robert T. Greene, 275 Pine Street. This ordinance is an attempt to solve a problem that I fear misses the point. The Mayor and Council can't see the forest for the trees. *Density* is the problem, *not* parked cars coming from elsewhere but overbuilding that's happening right here, right now, in town."

The audience erupts in a burst of private exchanges. He pauses to allow the noise to subside before continuing. "There's no regard for what's getting *built* here. And as a result, we don't have enough parking for our residents and businesses!"

Up until now the mayor has allowed Eddie to explain the crux of the ordinance. The councilman is doing a good job of educating the public on the need to pass it. But Robert Greene is another matter completely, and Joey draws the mike closer to make sure he is being heard. "The meeting was opened to the public for discussion of the parking ordinance. Perhaps you might like to weigh in on this matter and save your general observations for the end, when the public brings up anything they wish." Joey calculates that the delay will leave Greene fewer people in the audience for him to perform for.

Not so easily sidetracked, Robert pushes his point. "I think the two issues are inseparable, Mayor. Mr. Blauvelt is right. It didn't used to be a problem here in town."

Joey nods toward the old gentleman sitting in the audience. "I'm sure Mr. Blauvelt's recollections are accurate. But nowadays, more than one person in a family drives a car. Assuming, conservatively speaking, two cars per household, that's a lot of cars. The point of this ordinance is to free up spaces for those who live, work, and do business in town. Other towns have adopted ordinances similar to this with success. It is time we do so as well. Any more questions or comments?"

A far quieter murmur ripples through the audience this time. Flushed, the young man returns to his seat without another word. No one else steps forward to the mike to comment on this subject, and the public portion of the meeting concerning the ordinance closes. The council unanimously votes in favor of introducing the ordinance for a final vote at the next Mayor and Council meeting.

Robert, however, is not finished. When the meeting is opened to the public for general comments, he approaches the mike in front of the dais and identifies himself again for the public record.

"I am here to inquire about creating a new master plan and changing zoning for the DeVries property from mixed use to solely residential," he goes on. "Instead of two office buildings, which will bring us more traffic and parking headaches, making it even more impossible for residents to get in out of their driveways onto the road, why can't the parcel be re-zoned for ten single-family homes? This would reduce congestion and have the added benefit of increasing real estate values for all the other homes in the immediate area."

The idea of higher real estate values captures the interest of an audience that was beginning to get restless and eyeing the exit.

"The purchaser of the property," says the mayor, "has put forth a plan for two office buildings, which will bring in fresh ratables without putting undue stress on all the other services the town provides.

Besides benefitting from employment opportunities, those working there are likely to patronize our businesses. The more business ratables one has in town, the better it is for individual homeowners' tax bill."

"One can always find a way to cut taxes," offers Robert dismissively, in the manner of someone who has never had to balance a municipal budget. "The plan submitted has two buildings seven stories high. They will tower out of proportion to the rest of the area, blocking homeowners' access to sunshine. I'm concerned that we will be setting a precedent for developers to come with more plans for even taller rectangles, affecting the character of where we live."

"The height of the buildings will be taken under consideration by the Planning Board, Mr. Greene, of which you are a member and free to bring up your objections, to be discussed by the board and voted on. Until then, there is very little that this body can do. As for updating a master plan, it's an unnecessary expense when the current plan is not more than seven years old."

Robert decides not to pursue the subject any further at this meeting and takes his seat.

"Any further questions? Anybody?.... No? If that's the case, the public portion of the meeting is now closed and this mayor-and-council meeting has ended." Joey pounds the gavel twice.

Even though the meeting has officially ended, the public is in no hurry to leave, milling around, waiting for the opportunity to chat with the mayor or members of the council. Joey works the room but keeps an eye on the reporter questioning Greene about the need for a new master plan. As she is about to finish up, the young man casually mentions the skull in passing, asking the reporter whether she's been pursuing the story.

"I think there's something really fishy about the whole thing," he says. "So what if the house where it was found belongs to an esteemed member our local school system? There seems to be no real interest in getting to the bottom of this and finding out the truth. Who is being protected? And why?"

The reporter makes a mental note to follow up on that story the next day, before sidling over to ask the mayor a few questions about zoning.

Annie has by then planted herself in front of Robert. Her cheeks and nose are flush. It takes all the restraint she's learned in dealing with her mother's excesses not to clobber him over the head with her bag. "You've got a lot of nerve maligning my family with absolutely no evidence to back it up. We didn't even hide the matter from the law. Instead, *we* brought it *their* attention. We made no objection to our home being searched. We have submitted ourselves to countless questions, yet *you* continuously take cheap shots, insinuating the worst about us. And for what? To further a political career through innuendo? Is that the best you can do to get elected?"

Robert backs away, hands in the air to protect himself from the verbal assault. He attempts to hide his discomfort with a shrug. "I ask these questions because I believe in integrity. Rare in this day and age, I know—

"Integrity!" Annie shouts, silencing the room. "Is that what you call it. Well, two can play at this game. Better ask your family what happened to Sylvia. The one who *was* going to get married in my home, but didn't. There's a secret *there*, and I'm going to find out

what it is. And when I do, I will no longer be the *only* one with a skeleton in a closet. Except I never tried to hide mine."

Without saying another word, Robert makes his escape.

CHAPTER 16

EARLY THE NEXT MORNING, ISMENE IS RAKING leaves under the maple tree in the front yard when Rudy hails her, wishing her a good day as he crosses the street to chat. She leans the rake up against the tree and greets him in return.

He fingers the worn implement. "I remember raking leaves for your aunt. . .it took her such a long time to get over the initial shock of Bill's death. For months she rarely smiled, except politely for others' sake. Every day it was the same. She'd come home from school and tutor students. But she did little else. It was so unlike her to neglect yard work or the flower beds."

A wistful smile crosses his face before he continues, "I was maybe ten and head over heels in love with her. One day I screwed up my courage and came over to rake her lawn. I was humming 'Maple Leaf Rag' and dancing about when she pulled into the driveway. It was the first time I saw her old grin. Worth getting scolded by my mother—for having sneaked out of the house without letting her know where I was going—just to see Ginny brighten up even for a brief moment."

"'Maple Leaf Rag, really?" Ismene laughs. "How extraordinary. This tree makes me wnt to hum it, too. Do you think there's some magic going on?"

"With your aunt, anything is possible."

"She did have a starlike quality about her, didn't she?" Ismene smiles to herself before she continues. "Somehow, with her, everyday chores took on an air of wondrous importance." Ismene momentarily frowns. "When...when I wasn't at my best, Aunt Ginny would say, 'Chop wood, carry water. This is the way of the Tao,' to remind me that life's beautiful *and* wholly unexpected, so make of it what you will, even when peeling carrots."

He studies a bald patch in the grass. "Mm. She taught me the same through gardening. In caring for plants, they in turn take care of us."

Ismene breaks the momentary stillness that has settled over their memories by buttoning up her blue boiled-wool jacket and readjusting her green scarf. "Experience eventually showed me she was right. Nothing in this world is all that daunting that it can't be overcome with some flair, a bit of gratitude, and consistent endeavor."

"We are our own luck-smiths."

"We do, indeed, forge our own luck, don't we, Mr. Handelman."

"Please, call me Rudy."

Ismene continues as if she hasn't heard his request, wrapping the scarf even tighter around her neck. "Fall makes me wistful. It always reminds me that life is short and bittersweet."

To change the subject, she asks, "Seems to me that my aunt stole your heart forever. You never married, did you?"

"What I will admit, dear lady, is that I have a weakness for vibrant, beautiful women. And they very much run in your family."

She nods to acknowledge the compliment. "Please call me Ismene," she says, as she pulls off her gardening gloves, signaling that it's time to take a break from raking leaves. "Rudy, would you care for some tea?"

"I would indeed."

The two have settled across the harvest table in the kitchen, with cups of oolong and a plate of homemade peanut butter cookies between them, when Annie enters the room. She instantly hides her surprise with a winning smile, greeting Mr. Handelman with an upbeat good morning while grabbing a cup and saucer to join them. As she is about to sit down, she catches sight of her mother's arched eyebrow and adds a plate and cloth napkin. Once everything is appropriately arranged and a cup of tea is poured, she tells them about her run-in with Robert Greene.

"I'm afraid we won't be hearing the last of the skull story anytime soon," she glumly concludes. "Not as long as he intends to run against Joey Samartino for mayor."

Rudy shakes his head. "This nonsense will never outlast your Aunt Ginny's good name or truly tarnish yours, Annie."

"I didn't," Ismene sighs, "see any reason to go to the police in the first place."

Annie opens her mouth to protest.

"But—" Ismene has raised her hand— "now that it's done, I wouldn't bother about what people say. Most gossip is senseless entertainment for the very bored or the very stupid. In either case, their opinions don't amount to much. My advice to you—though you don't seem to value it much these days—is to ignore it, and the gossip will eventually go away."

"But it's not *right*."

"No, it is not," snaps Ismene, placing her cup on its saucer to give her time to regroup. She shakes her head and tries again in a softened voice. "You are one of the kindest people I know, Annie. Robert Greene, poor creature, is a bit of a buffoon at his very best. I am going to ask you a question—why are you kind, Annie? Are you kind because you expect people to be kind to you in return? Or do you behave the way you do because it's the only way you know how?"

Annie sips her tea. "Well, I do wish that people would be more considerate."

"Yes, darling, but this is not a Hallmark card moment that I'm asking you to contemplate. Would I be wrong to say your commitment to having a gentle heart *is* who you are, and nothing could change your behavior for the worse no matter what?"

Annie shrugs. "Not sure how to answer that."

"Oh? Then let's take Lara Snow as an example. An airhead extraordinaire."

"Mom, don't be so judgmental."

"That's my point, Mouse. She's calculating, makes a move on Andrew in your presence, and you still aren't comfortable with calling her the stupid cow that she is."

"Mom, please stop!"

"Can you tell me I'm wrong?"

Annie fidgets in her chair. "I'd rather not say!"

"No, you'd rather not, because you have a huge heart. So why should you care what fools say about you?"

"In this matter," Rudy interrupts before an argument ensues, "I agree with your mother."

Annie looks at him mournfully and grabs a cookie.

Rudy quickly adds, "I say this only because it is exactly what your aunt Ginny repeatedly taught, whether I was in her classroom or her garden. What is good is true and, therefore, will survive." He turns to address Ismene. "I loved your aunt because she taught me to trust what I see with my eyes and feel with my heart, and let that beauty pull me through tough times."

Ismene, rubbing her temples, shifts gears. "I know things are going well between you and your father. And that is how I want it. But for the sake of your sanity and mine in regard to the skull, I want you to consider what I'm about to say. In small towns, where everyone knows everyone else's business, do you think your father's behavior remained secret for long?"

Annie breaks the cookie in half to stall. "I guess not," she whispers, eyes remaining on the two halves.

"Annie, look at me."

The girl looks up and takes a bite of cookie.

"I'm not trying to stir up trouble between the two of you. But I *am* trying to tell you from experience that I had to live down a lot of gossip by forging ahead and being me—living as I pleased, head held high with no excuses and no explanations."

Annie's hazel eyes widen as she stares at her mother. It has never dawned on her, even since learning the truth about her parents, that maybe Ismene's impossible behavior has always been defensive, a way to survive all the hurt she has been dealt.

AT BOROUGH HALL THAT SAME MORNING, Joey and John are sitting across from one another at Kelly's desk, sipping their indifferent coffee, when the borough clerk casually says, "I have to hand it to that Clairmont girl. She showed spunk last night the way she took on Greene."

"Yeah." Joey stares at his paper coffee cup, refusing to say anything more.

"Wish I knew what she was hinting at."

Joey sighs, sits up, and puts his empty cup on the desk. "I don't know for sure, so I don't want to step in it, but there's been some talk that one of the Ahearn sisters, way back when, was supposed to get married and didn't. Or at the very least no one knows for sure. And she may have been pregnant to boot."

John, expecting more to follow, waits in silence until it's obvious Joey isn't going to continue. ". . .And?"

"And?" Joey shrugs. "Nothing! Not that I blame the girl for being furious with the little prick. But I don't have the luxury of punching him out physically or emotionally. Instead I must *entertain—and* answer the question, 'How do I wish to comport myself as a seasoned, elected official, running for re-election?'"

"The adult in the room?"

"Right. This rising above it all is supposed to express some crap about my living legacy. Or so my mother tells me. If my behavior even hints at being as small-minded as him, I'd end up failing to teach the next generation of politicians how to be a *mensch*, as well as looking like a complete idiot to our voting public."

John gives his boss a sideways glance. "Is that what's eating you?"

Joey changes the subject. "You know, I haven't thought about this in ages, but I first met Ginny Spencer when I was four. My pop was taking on odd jobs during the weekends for extra money. He did some painting and repairs around her house. Johnny and I tagged along when my mother brought Pop some lunch that first day. We spotted two bikes in the driveway. Pop had left them there as he was clearing out her garage. Ginny allowed us to play with them, and then she let us *keep* them."

For a moment Joey looks out the office window and studies the billowy white clouds drifting by at a clip against a bright blue sky. "She was a nice woman. I hope to hell that the medical examiner's office gives us a report soon. Maybe it'll bring the matter to a graceful end."

John, having coaxed Joey to talk about the pink elephant in the room, returns to the business at hand—preparing for the next Mayor and Council meeting.

ROBERT GREENE LEANS TOWARD the breakfast table, cupping one hand under his chin, as the other taps against the tabletop. That Clairmont girl gave him a scare last night, he thinks as he studies the last bite of toast with peanut butter untouched on his plate. What if there is some family secret that he doesn't know about? His mother has so many brothers and sisters. Each has had three, four, or five kids. And the next generation seems to be following suit. He always thought it was safer not to pay attention to what his mother said when she was in one of her vindictive moods. Ignorance as protective cover has enabled him, when necessary, to navigate family landmines that he's always sensed were there but hidden. So maybe there is something he's overlooked or only half-heard when she—who could drone on and on—listed her well-preserved family dissatisfactions.

He calls Kathy to let her know he'll be a bit late and heads over to see his mother.

It was Harriet's turn to host Lara. The two women—laughing over cups of coffee, having just finished their eggs and toast—greet Robert with delight.

Lara notices him undressing her with his eyes and excuses herself to go change. He's momentarily distracted as she leaves the room, following the movement of her hips in the thin cotton pajamas she's wearing. He makes note of the fact that she looks as good without makeup as she does with it. When Harriet again asks whether or not he's hungry, he tears himself away from where his mind is drifting and shakes his head.

Harriet listens, lips compressed into a thin line, about the exchange with the Clairmont girl.

"How *dare* she suggest that we have anything to hide. We are a respectable family. Pay our bills and keep out of trouble." She grabs the empty plates and drops them into the sink with a clatter. Standing with her back to her son, arms folded, she adds, "For heaven sakes, you have one uncle who is a police chief and another who's a judge. No one in our family has ever gone to jail." She slams her fist against the counter. "The *nerve* of her to threaten us with digging into our past."

Robert, an old hand at navigating his mother's furies, retorts, "I know we come from fine and hardy stock. I'm just as proud to be an Ahearn as I am to be a Greene, if not more." He waits, but his mother makes no reply. "But, Ma, if there is something that we'd rather not have anybody know, now is the time to tell me."

The short, plump woman turns abruptly around in silent fury, finds her voice, and shouts, "Are you stupid, or can't you hear? I *told* you, we have nothing, *nothing* to hide."

Filled with alarm, Robert changes the subject, cutting the visit short by telling her he has just remembered that he has an appointment and must rush to get there on time. As he takes his leave, he decides to get hold of Uncle Bobby, the only person in the family from whom he has half a chance to getting a straight answer on the subject.

CHAPTER 17

L ATER THAT EVENING, ROBERT PARKS IN FRONT of his
uncle's home. His aunt takes him directly into the study—
a room completely lined with bookshelves—and shuts the
door.

Even with books cramming every shelf, the room remains meticulously ordered. The furniture is sparing, two club chairs facing a
desk making the study look bigger than it is. The judge, who has
been writing on a yellow legal pad, looks over his glasses and drawls,
"Let me guess. . .you didn't take my advice about the skull."

Robert sinks onto one of the chairs and avoids his uncle's piercing glance by reading the titles of several first editions on the shelves
behind the desk, then shrugs.

The judge lays his pen down. "What is it you want to know?"

"The girl with the skull on the roof says we have some dirty secret to hide, and she's going to find it."

"And why did she threaten to do that?"

Robert merely licks his lips and doesn't answer.

"Don't play games with me, young man. And don't waste my time." He leans back in his chair, folding his arms over his chest, and waits for his nephew to give him an answer.

Robert hates it when his uncle brings him up short. When he was growing up, his mother sometimes asked her younger brother to step in and "talk to the boy!" Then Robert had to endure a lengthy lecture about doing better in order to aspire to a life of probity. It's bad enough he never can earn his mother's approval; Uncle Bob has a way of making him feel like a worm without ever saying it. "I was talking to a reporter. The Clairmont girl overheard me tell her that the skull story is probably a good one and she should look into it."

"Tell her? Tell *her?*" Bob exhales. "Oh, boy." He takes a few breaths and tries to calm down, reminding himself that his nephew has no father to speak of and a shrew for a mother. It's no wonder he hasn't any sense at all. "Were you preening for a female reporter, Robert?"

"I—what?"

"You heard me. Do you know the reporter, trust her to be fair?"

Robert is confused. "Know the reporter? Yeah. I mean, I've seen her around at the meetings, and I've talked to her before."

The judge places both palms on his desk, rolls forward, and takes another deep breath. "Okay, Robert, let me rephrase the question. Were you not thinking at all, risking the *appearance* of slanderous talk? Or were you just not thinking *and* also showing off because you were talking to a woman?"

"Showing off? No, no! I was just getting my story out."

"Think, Robert," Bob growls. "Would you have said the same

thing if the reporter had been male?"

Robert's eyes widen. He hesitates only a moment before shaking his head.

"One of the worst things you can do—what can cause you more grief than your worst enemy, is to discount a woman's worth with careless talk." Bob slaps the desk in frustration. "You better hope that reporter, if she follows up on the story, doesn't skewer you as a result of what she finds."

Robert sinks deeper into the chair and remains silent.

Bob tries again. "You'd be doing yourself a favor—and you'd be far more appealing to the opposite sex—if you stopped behaving as if you were God's gift to women. While you *are* capable and good-looking, you are no Adonis, my boy, no matter what you think!"

Red-faced, Robert looks away from his uncle but says nothing.

"Now, what *did* that girl say to you that you are now here asking about family history?"

"Something about one of my aunts, about a marriage that didn't take place."

"Ah!" Bob wonders what information he can trust his nephew with. He yawns, suddenly feeling very tired as he always does when facing certain matters about his family. "Sylvia's fiancé died in an accident right before the wedding. To complicate matters, she was pregnant at the time. His family offered to take her back to Oklahoma and, when Ellen was born, to raise her as Crocker."

"Who's Ellen?"

"Lara's mother." By now, Bob is wishing he had a bourbon to drink. "I don't know how keen an observer of human nature you are, but it's not uncommon to find that, if one generation has a pregnancy out of marriage, the next—though it's never a given—may follow suit. This was the case with Ellen, who also got pregnant out of wedlock. In that instance, the couple married, but Ellen died giving birth. Lara's father eventually remarried, and Lara quickly became an inconvenience—leaving his daughter to be raised by Sylvia," he concludes, deciding that less information is the best way to handle his nephew.

"I don't understand," muses Robert. "What's this got to do with me?"

"Having had a relatively easier life than your mother, you wouldn't understand. But when you grow up poor, respectability is something you crave. Your mother was born during the Depression, and she was the second youngest in a household filled with children, so she wanted respectability more than most, and she still does."

Bob watches his nephew mentally assess the damage to himself as minimal, and is relieved when Robert, rather than pursuing the matter, dismisses it with a nod of thanks and a handshake as he takes his leave.

ANDREW IS SITTING IN HIS UNCLE'S living room, wondering what Annie is doing at this moment in her home across the street. Having followed through with his promise to find out what he could about the mysterious wedding, he's still hoping to get more information than he's gotten so far from his uncle.

Rudy shuts his eyes as if trying to force memories up with a grimace. He opens them. "Wait! I vaguely remember that we—your grandparents, your mother, and me—were visiting relatives somewhere in New York State when *something* happened that had the entire neighborhood talking."

"Do you remember what or when?"

Rudy shakes his head. "I never paid much attention to adults' gossip. Back then children would go to school, then disappear outside and play till it was time to come home for dinner and homework. Adults lived in a separate universe, like vast ships on distant horizons.

"I would imagine, however, if the brouhaha was about a wedding, it most likely would have occurred either late in '45 or in '46, when our boys were returning from the war. There were many weddings then. And if you count backwards from a probable wedding date, my guess is that Sylvia Ahearn was Ginny's student around 1944."

Andrew is clearly disappointed. "But I thought you spent a lot of time with Ginny Spencer."

"I most certainly did. She tutored me for years till I outgrew my asthma. I also went over to help her in the garden whenever I had a chance, because we discussed important things like trees, flowers, bees, and water. But while my love for Ginny never dimmed, I did outgrow my crush as a teenager, when my attention was drawn elsewhere."

It has never occurred to Andrew that his uncle is anything but a dyed-in-the-wool bachelor. He hesitates before venturing to say, "You sound wistful, Uncle Rudy."

"In a way, yes." The older man stares at the lights coming from the Spencer home and wonders how the Clairmont women are faring. "Of course, it's sad, letting go of childhood—especially when it was, on the whole, a happy one." Rudy leans forward to meet his nephew's gaze. "But necessary in order to scale the walls of manhood."

He allows the silence to settle, noticing Andrew giving him a sidelong glance—a sign of his full attention. "I knew early on that being a gardener would be my life's work. That I'd built my passion into a healthy business was not a given when I started out as a young man. But I had faith in the healing capacity of Nature, and dedicated my life to taking care of gardens.

"Still, though it is hard to believe now, I *was* once a young man." Rudy again closes his eyes for a moment and sighs. "I fell in love. But my prospects were not considered good enough at the time, and she spurned me." He looks away for a moment before facing his nephew to continue, "In love I wasn't as courageous or as determined as I was in my work. So I turned inward, and before I knew it, decades had flown by, and I suddenly found myself very much alone."

"Who was the girl, Uncle Rudy?"

"My foe all through grammar school. Slowly, however, I began to see the good in her, and in high school we fell in love, Harriet Ahearn and I."

Andrew's jaw drops. "Robert Greene's mother? Are you kidding me?"

"It can happen, you know. Someone you saw as your antagonist can very unexpectedly become your friend."

Andrew considers the rocky start he's had with Annie Clairmont.

"While it's true there are times in life one should be reasonable, even cautious," his uncle goes on, "when it comes to love, hedging one's bets nearly always leads to regret."

Rudy again waits till the dust settles before he goes on. "Harriet married a dentist destined to be wealthy. She chose to enter a loveless contract. And when her marriage ended, her anger scorched her heart so much that love was no longer possible for her."

"...What a terrible thing. What a waste."

"Yes, and from what I've observed from a distance, it is her youngest child and only son Robert who has had to carry the burden of her bitterness."

Andrew becomes indignant. "That doesn't excuse his behavior."

"No, it does not. Ultimately, we are responsible for our choices. But isn't that what I'm saying? Like the leaves on a tree, we come and go—bright in the spring, strong in the summer, glorious in the fall, until eventually we feel the twinge of winter creeping in. Whether we wither and die, choking on sorrow, or take solace in the joy we've created is up to us. I have lived my life simply, working with my hands and doing what I love. But having lived it being afraid to get hurt again in love was an enormous blunder I now regret."

Having given this some thought, Andrew quietly asks, "Are you saying that I'm hedging my bets?"

"...I know you have your reasons, Andy. But there comes a time to take account. Regret isn't so terrible if it pushes you toward something better. Otherwise, you end up like poor Harriet, who thinks she knows everything, full of blind certainty that leaves no room for love to blossom. You have to ask yourself, How open am I to fresh possibilities?"

Andrew hugs his uncle before taking his leave. Once the door shuts behind him, he pauses at the top of the steps, wondering what to do next. It's a clear, bright night. Looking up at the moon that's beginning to wane, he thinks about the risk of ending up alone for fear of being hurt. Isn't that what Jack tried to tell him in his own loyal bulldog way not so long ago at CJ's?

He sighs, envious of his friend's bliss. But he's also *well* aware that not everyone is as lucky as Jack and Rachel. He's seen more than a few marriages that friends had plunged into while in their mid-twenties dissolve into bitter divorce by thirty. He looks across the street for signs of life in the Clairmont home. No one is in the front parlor or dining room. They're probably in the kitchen, washing and drying dishes at this time of the night. He shakes his head. These are not typical women, and life within their orbit will never be boring, that's for sure.

He decides it's still early enough to ring Christina Hill's doorbell to see if he can't make more sense of the story. Glancing again at the moon, he crosses the street to call on Annie to join him.

Christina is delighted to see the two young people. She invites them in and asks whether they will join her in a homemade ice-cream sundae—vanilla ice cream, hot fudge, and multi-colored sprinkles.

The three are sitting in the kitchen, navigating the hot fudge so it won't slide off the ice cream dish onto the table, when Christina asks, "So what brings you here?"

Annie hands her the photo. Christina puts on her reading glasses, which are attached to a chain of Venetian-glass hexagons around her neck, and stares at the picture for a long while before answering. "Yes, I remember. The girl standing next to Ginny is an Ahearn. Sarah—no, *Sylvia*—was her name. Never liked her much."

Annie's eyes fly open. "Really? Why?"

"I couldn't understand why Ginny took her on. Even more so,

how she grew *fond* of her. I think Ginny was lonely with both her dad and Bill gone. Somehow Ginny, who's nobody's fool, was oblivious to the girl's deep resentment toward her." Christina pours more hot fudge on her ice cream to completely cover her three small scoops. "I'd catch Sylvia, when she thought no one was looking, with a really bitter look on her face. And while Ginny managed to give her a genteel exterior, you can't change a tiger's stripes when the tiger refuses to do what's necessary for real change—which is change from the inside out. . . ."

Christina shakes her head. "Sylvia was the kind of girl who would gleefully backstab even a person who helped her if it would further her interests. Her heart was fueled by jealousy—and that jealousy, in my opinion, was aimed at your great-aunt."

No one speaks for a while as they consume mouthfuls of dessert.

Frowning, Annie asks, "Was it a money issue?"

"Oh," Christina laughs, "it went much farther than *that*. If Sylvia had been a millionaire, her feelings toward your aunt wouldn't have changed, not one bit. It was Ginny's open heart that she envied more than anything."

"What about some wedding happening at Annie's home?" Andrew follows Christina's example and pours more fudge on his ice cream, tossing on a spoonful of sprinkles to make his sundae look festive.

Christina suddenly becomes very quiet and concentrates on finishing her ice cream. Andrew and Annie exchange glances, aware of the sudden shift in temperature.

Christina shrugs. "Sorry, I can't be of more help.

CHAPTER 18

EARLY THE NEXT MORNING IT'S RAINING with a vengeance. Annie, consuming her sundae last night, got some chocolate on her favorite shirt, and she's washing it, along with a couple of other things, before the stain sets. As she returns to the basement to put her wet clothing into the dryer, she finds that her mother has left some of her sweaters in there, dry but now in need of being pressed.

In a good mood, she quickly touches them up with the iron and folds them. She runs up the two flights of stairs and makes her way into her mother's room to lay the sweaters on top of others neatly stacked in the dresser drawer where Ismene keeps them. About to shut the drawer, the girl spots a number of old letters, tied in a faded blue ribbon, half hidden to one side. Unable to resist, she glances at the names on the envelopes. The letters were addressed to Ginny Spencer, and they came from Buddy Crocker. She stares at them for a while before realizing this is what she's been looking for, hidden all this time in her mother's dresser drawer.

When Ismene returns from her morning chores—getting her hair trimmed and food shopping—she finds Annie in the parlor, sitting cross-legged on the wingback chair with the letters strewn all over the coffee table. Alma is dozing in Annie's lap.

Lips instantly compressed, Ismene hangs her damp raincoat in the hall closet and disappears into the kitchen to put her purchases away. When she returns, she dryly remarks, "I see that I didn't do a very good job teaching you to respect other people's privacy."

Annie retorts, "These don't belong to you. They belonged to Aunt Ginny. Since you must have found them somewhere in this house, and I own the house, by default they belong to me."

Folding her arms across her chest, Ismene flushes bright red and growls, "Really, you're impossible."

"*I'm* impossible! Is that all you've got to say?" Annie snaps. "I'm doing my best to find out what actually happened to clear our name, and you've hidden the truth from me, *again.*"

"Oh, don't be so melodramatic!" Ismene shouts back. Lowering her voice to a more civil register, she continues, "What I mean to say is that these letters are Aunt Ginny's business, not ours. And she deserves the right to take some secrets to her grave, just like everyone else who lives and breathes on this Earth."

"...Where did you find them, anyway?" Annie waves the letter she's just finished reading, already ashamed of having lorded over her mother the fact that she owns the house, but still furious that they've been hidden from her.

Alma yawns, jumps off Annie's lap, makes her way to Ismene, and circles the distraught woman, rubbing her thick fur against Ismene's ankles as a reminder that naps solve every problem except maybe an empty stomach. Ismene bends down to pet the cat, who has at last come to accept her as part of the family—though her daughter remains her favorite.

"I mean it, Annie. I really mean it when I say that Aunt Ginny *wanted* to keep these letters a secret." Ismene takes a seat across from her daughter. "...A while ago, Alma knocked over a vase filled with flowers from a side table in the study. By the time I got something to wipe up the mess, a matter of moments, the water had disappeared. It took some doing, but I located a floorboard that had been loosened. I pried it open, and I found a locked metal box below. The key was in a tiny wooden box, hiding in plain sight on the bookshelf. The letters were inside. It seems to me that Aunt Ginny went to a great deal of trouble to hide them. And, therefore, her wishes should be respected."

Annie thinks about this for a moment. "Yeah, but we have them anyway."

"And have you read anything earth-shattering?"

"Not really," Annie reluctantly admits. "I mean, they're not love letters. But she and Buddy sound awfully close."

"That's exactly what I thought when I read them. They're intimate, but they're the letters of friends, not lovers. Still—" Ismene exhales, picking up one of the letters from the coffee table, and stares at it— "I can't help thinking there's something more than meets the eye about them. Otherwise, why hide them?"

"You mean maybe they *did* fall in love?"

"Falling in love exchanging letters! That's a thought." Ismene shrugs. "Who knows? Stranger things have happened. But I'm not so sure we will ever know the truth, now that Aunt Ginny is gone. *Or* that it's our business to find out."

They sit in silence for a while before Annie gives voice to her misgivings. "Maybe we *do* know. Maybe neither one of us wants to admit the possibility that Aunt Ginny loved a man involved with another woman. And kept the letters because it was the only thing she had left of that relationship. Otherwise, as you say, why bother hiding them?"

Neither speaks for a while. Annie suddenly asks, "Did you know Granny Grace remembers that Sylvia and Buddy were supposed to have gotten married in this house?"

Ismene shakes her head.

"Granny Grace once teased Aunt Ginny about being sweet on Buddy, and Aunt Ginny denied it. Apparently, she insisted that the couple get married here in this house. But when I asked Mrs. Hill last night, she had no information. Mr. Handelman couldn't help either. He said he was too young then to be paying attention to adult things like weddings."

". . . You spoke to Christina and Rudy about this?"

"Actually, Andrew spoke to his uncle, and we spoke to Mrs. Hill."

Ismene arches a brow.

Annie rushes to explain, "I asked Andrew to help me get to the bottom of this story. He knows a lot of people in town, and I. . .I thought he could help. But so far, we've found nothing that brings clarity to the situation."

"What makes you think any of this is pertinent?"

"Andrew asked the same question. I'm not sure at all. It's just that I've got no other leads to follow. So today is as good a day as any to go to the library and find out, one way or the other, whether this wedding is a dead end or not."

It's mid-afternoon when John Kelly notices that the rain has finally stopped. He decides to take a break, having worked through the lunch hour, and hurries over to the library to return some books. The wind is still blowing, the sun mostly hidden behind lowering clouds, and though the library is only three short blocks away, he's grateful to get out of the cold. As he bounds up the staircase to drop his books into the return bin near the reception desk, he catches sight of Annie Clairmont out of the corner of his eye. She's sitting at a microfilm carrel.

Curious, he approaches. "Well, young lady, you look like you could use a break."

She rubs her eyes. "Hello, Mr. Kelly. How are you liking the lapsang you bought?"

He grins. "It's my new favorite. I've become a fan of brewing pots of tea at home."

She sits back in her chair and sighs. "I sure could do with some myself just about now. I've been here for a while with no luck."

"What exactly are you looking for, if I may ask?"

"You may." She grins. "Though I'm beginning to suspect it's probably a fool's errand, I'm scanning all weddings and engagement announcements after the end of World War II, looking for one in particular."

"And you haven't found it."

"Not in the latter half of 1945. But I've just started 1946. And there were a lot more local papers back then, so if I don't find it in this paper, there are a few others to go to."

"...This have anything to do with Robert Greene?"

"In a roundabout way," she answers reluctantly, then shakes her head. "No," she replies firmly. "Not really. I started looking for answers to clear our name. But now it's about giving my aunt her due. I hope, once I've pieced the story together, it will make her completely human—full of wisdom and mistakes, accidental kindnesses and acts of sacrifice for love, all of it—rather than a merely saintly, good woman who worked hard to help educate generations of kids."

Annie laughs, embarrassed to admit to anyone, let alone a near stranger, what she's about to say. "And since we have an unidentified skull to thank for this opportunity to complete a picture, I feel— well, to be totally honest—I feel like the Egyptian goddess Isis, who puts Osiris back together after he's been killed and torn to pieces. Whoever the skull belongs to, *and* Aunt Ginny, have both been torn to pieces, and they deserve to rest in peace."

He remains quiet for a while. He finally says, "I'm sure you must be aware that not everyone will be pleased with this."

She shrugs. "Sure. My mother's first on the list. But lately I've been confronted with the cost of family secrets. How they shape the lives of those who keep them and those who are kept from them. The cost of that silence is terrible."

Admiring such forthrightness, John answers in kind. "Very true. But most people don't have your courage, and they won't regard seeking out the truth as an act of healing. At best, they'll see it as. . . inconvenient."

"I know. But don't acts of courage happen when there's no other option left?"

He studies her earnest face looking up at him, smiles, and reaches into his pocket to hand her his card. "When this is all over, you give me a call and we'll talk some more. Okay?"

She looks the card over and nods.

He pats her on the shoulder and leaves, certain he's just met the person he wants to replace him one day at work.

LARA SNOW FLIPS HER MAGAZINE SHUT with a sigh. She hates being bored. Robert's been unavailable for three days, with work and a Planning Board meeting demanding his full attention. Aunt Harriet, with whom she's been thick as thieves, has—since her son came and went during that breakfast—been in an ugly mood that hasn't lifted yet. Unable to figure out what happened, Lara's in the dark and doesn't like it.

Nothing seemed to be amiss that morning. Aware of Robert's eyes scanning her body under her pajamas at the breakfast table, she'd hurried to change into jeans and a tight black sweater, hoping to make him sit up and take notice, enough to finally invite her over to his place. It'd taken her no time to change, but when she made her entrance, rouged, coiffed, and heavily scented, to her astonishment he'd already left.

Perhaps she misjudged the situation. Perhaps she should have continued to allow him to undress her with his eyes, maybe even helped things along by "accidentally" brushing her toe against his calf beneath the table, right under Aunt Harriet's nose. That would have driven him to the brink and forced him to make the next move while he tried to keep his composure in front of his mother. The last few times they've gone out, she's caught that hard look on his face, the one some men get when they want a woman.

Lara has been in no rush. And has enjoyed reeling in her cousin like a recalcitrant trout. She knows that he's far too cautious to commit to anyone but himself. So she is taking her time, slowly coaxing him to a point of recklessness. Then he'll become hers. It's the selfish ones, once caught, that capitulate utterly and completely as long as they get all the attention they crave. A diamond ring from Robert would be her ticket out of Oklahoma. Aunt Harriet has hinted more than once that that outcome would be just fine with her.

But Lara hasn't seen Robert since that morning, making it difficult for her to gauge the situation and choose her next move.

And while she's gone alone into the city to wander through a couple of museums and photography galleries as well as do some shopping, none of it amuses her as much as dressing for parties or going out on a date. Let's face it, Lara thinks, what's the fun in doing anything if there isn't someone there to admire you while you do it?

She takes a walk to consider her next move. While window-shopping down Main Street, she spots Annie Clairmont heading to the Little Shop. Lara grins and picks up her pace in order to bump into her as they both reach the front door. "Oh, my," she oozes, "what a surprise to find you here."

Annie, reluctant to show she isn't as pleased to see Lara, replies, "Well, um, I suppose if anyone wants a good cup of coffee or tea, this is the place to come."

"Oh, yes, I love the coffee here."

"I'm a fan of the tea."

Lara looks at Annie expectantly but doesn't respond. The silence grows. Annie finally asks, "How has your family visit been going?"

"Great." Lara smiles. "I've just about visited with every aunt, uncle, and cousin I have on this side of my family. I'm so happy to finally have met them all. Such terrific people, but that's what I'd expect from my grandmother's family. I must say, I've found the people here are so friendly in general. You wouldn't think it possible with New York just the other side of the river."

It's Annie's turn to say nothing and allow the awkwardness to settle. As she reaches for the door, Lara gushes, "Look, there's one small table in the corner where we can sit and have a chat over our coffee and tea."

Annie agrees, hoping that information will flow in both directions.

Once they're seated at the tiny table that barely has any room for anything besides two beverages, Annie asks, "You said you spent a lot of time with your grandmother?"

For a moment Lara's smile vanishes. She forces herself to smile once again and continues, "Yes, my mother died when I was born. My father traveled a lot and left me in my grandmother's care. And while I grew up surrounded by my grandfather's family—lots of farmers and teachers—and from time to time actually lived with them, it was my grandmother who raised me."

Annie studies her cup of tea, realizing that she has more in common with Lara than she ever could have imagined. Feeling guilty for having unreasonably judged her merely for being so very beautiful, she forces herself to face the girl and murmurs, "I know what it's like to grow up with a family member missing from your life. My father...traveled a lot, too. I didn't see him for many years. And I spent a lot of time with my aunt Ginny growing up. She was as special to me as your grandmother is to you, for pretty much the same reason."

Lara continues to smile, but at that moment her hatred for Annie has crystalized. How *dare* she feel sorry for her. How *dare* she indulge herself by thinking they were alike, and, worse, making her feel momentarily vulnerable and needy—feelings she learned to ignore completely once puberty hit and she understood how to use her looks to get what she wanted. Whatever it takes, she will get even with this hoity-toity girl who thinks she understands *anything* about her life. Coyly she asks, "And how is that dishy photographer of yours doing?"

Annie stammers, "I. . .I don't know what you're talking about. If you mean Andrew, he's not my *anything*."

"Oh, you mean he's a free agent? Good to know. Then you won't mind my taking a crack at getting him."

"I see." Annie stares at Lara, her temper simmering. "You think people can be acquired and, I suppose, discarded at will."

Lara, startled by the disapproving look on the other's face, is about to object, but Annie, now angry, plows on. "While I've come to understand no one is perfect, that people are far too complicated to be solely one thing or another, I know in my heart that everyone has the right to be treated with dignity. That means trust." Annie scans the girl's confused face and despairs. "Trust means allowing relationships to flourish with time, rather than treating them like chess pieces on a game board."

Lara continues to stare at her as if she were speaking Chinese.

Annie momentarily wavers but sees that the situation is hopeless. She shivers, though the shop is quite warm, and silently takes her leave.

CHAPTER 19

LARA BLOTS HER LIPS, looks in the mirror, and decides to apply a bit more lipstick in a deeper shade of red. This time the color and intensity are just right. She fingers the lace that trims the top of her black stockings, then adjusts herself to best advantage in the black-lace bustier she's wearing. She has the matching garter belt and panties on as well.

Her undergarments have cost a small fortune but are worth it: She's going to turn up the heat to see how far she can push Robert. Stepping into a short black dress and slipping into black high heels, she faces the mirror, casually turning this way and that to see how far she must move to show a bit of that lace.

Not that she'll let him get very far, not tonight. She's not in a forgiving mood. He's taken his time to ask her out again—a whole week since the breakfast fiasco. She pins up her long blonde hair, tugging one or two strands out of place. Looking in the mirror once again, she smiles, satisfied with her plans to make him suffer a bit—maybe even a lot.

The Lion's Club is giving a dinner, along with a silent auction, at a fancy catering hall to raise money for local families in need. She will not have his undivided attention. Robert will be pressing the flesh to gather support for his campaign. But two can play that game. She remembers how unnerved he got when Aunt Elaine promised to introduce her to eligible men. Confident she can make more than one man turn to look at her tonight, Lara will teach him a lesson he won't forget.

THOUGH ISMENE AND ANNIE ARE Rudy and Andrew's guests at the dinner, Ismene has insisted on buying tickets for herself and her daughter in order to support the *fête*, and hands them with a flourish to the woman taking the tickets. They check their coats at the end of the hallway, scan the table where place cards are listed in alphabetical order to find the table they have been assigned, then turn their attention to the room where the cocktail hour and auction have been set up.

Tables covered with green cloths bear an assortment of gift baskets set up on stands with fall foliage in orange, yellow, and red around them, all surrounded by webs of tiny orange lights suggesting a fairytale landscape.

A waitress presents mother and daughter—both wearing their little black dresses and heels—with a tray of miniature quiches, and each chooses one. Another waiter offers them wine. Sipping a white, Ismene is excited to see a local travel agent is offering one of the new river cruises on the Rhine through the Netherlands, France, and Germany; she makes a bid, thinking how nice it would be, after visiting her ex in Rotterdam, to travel through Europe on a river cruise.

She also notices that Le Mangoire is offering dinner for four, and enters her name and an amount that exceeds the most recent bid by rather a lot.

Annie has in the meantime spied a basket from the Little Shop filled with her favorite chocolates and an interesting sample of teas and coffees. She's about to place a bid when Andrew, in a three-piece charcoal suit and maroon-and-navy rep tie not fully yanked into place, appears at her side.

"Enjoying yourself, I hope?" he asks with a smile.

"Oh, yes! It's fun to see what everyone in town has offered to help out." She giggles, straightening his tie. "You clean up pretty well, too, you know!"

"Ah, thank you, ma'am." He adds, "My uncle is offering free lawn care for six months."

"I'll make sure to place a bid for that," answers Ismene. "Just show me where the basket is."

Andrew points her in the right direction and turns back to Annie. "I'm sorry that duty calls and I won't be able to direct all my attention to you. There's always something that has to be done at the last minute. But I trust you'll enjoy yourself."

Robert has meanwhile entered the room with Lara on his arm. He spots a knot of men standing close to the bar—lawyers with whom Uncle Bob frequently socializes. As he shifts to head in that direction, Lara asks, "Would you be a dear and bring me a whiskey? I see some friends over there in the corner I'd like to say hello to."

Robert, eager to make his way to the power brokers, absent-mindedly nods his consent without seeing where Lara is pointing.

She makes her way toward Annie and Andrew. "Why, hello.

How great it is to find you both here." Glancing at Annie, she adds, "I wouldn't think such an event would interest you, except maybe for the *prizes* in the room."

Without waiting for Annie's response, she turns to Andrew, moving so she nearly screens her opponent's view, and purrs, "How come you're not here with your equipment?"

Andrew shrugs. "I'm working in another capacity tonight, organizing volunteers."

Surveying the room, Lara leans closer toward Andrew and playfully whispers, "Bet you'd have plenty of photographic subjects in this venue. I mean, take a look at that bald fat man two tables over writing his bid down, licking his lips. Or the little old lady standing alone by the door, glancing left and right to make sure no one notices her take another glass of wine." With a giggle, she resumes her normal speaking voice. "We reveal ourselves despite how hard we try not to. Don't you think?"

He manages to keep a straight face. "I give you there are more than a few possibilities in the room."

She offers a conspiratorial wink. "I must confess, I have a weakness for fashion photographers like Avedon and Irving Penn. Making women look like works of art is such a gift."

"Don't forget the women in the field," Andrew replies. "Annie Leibovitz, Dorothea Lange, Margaret Bourke-White before her. Very powerful work."

"I'm from Oklahoma, so we've all grown up seeing those Lange pictures of families suffering during the Dust Bowl. It's part of our history. Just like Curtis's portraits of plains Indians."

"His work makes me sad when I look at it," says Andrew. "Proud people losing their way of life."

"Is that what you see?" Lara shakes her head. "I see a defiant people who keep their strength under wraps no matter what's happening externally. Well-hidden secrets, which they tap into when needed. But I guess that's the point of great art. Two people look at the same image and get different responses."

At that moment Robert shows up with Lara's drink. He nods to Andrew and Annie and says, "I couldn't find you. Thought I'd lost you."

Lara thanks Robert as she accepts her glass. No one speaks for moment or two. She allows Robert's awkwardness to sink in before proceeding. "Andrew and I were just discussing photography." She grins at Andrew, pleased to see Robert getting beet-red in the face. "It's a passion of mine. In fact, I plan to visit the International Center for Photography next week and would *love* to get a professional's point of view. Would you consider going with me?" she asks Andrew.

He looks over her shoulder and asks Annie, "Interested in visiting the ICP?"

Annie smiles back, surprised that she's more amused than bothered by Lara's antics, with which she has become all too familiar. "Love to. Never been there."

Robert stares at the three, flabbergasted. Almost as if it were a second thought, Lara purrs, "You can come, too, Robert, that is if you're not too busy."

Across the room Ismene has been chatting with Rudy when John Kelly approaches them with a warm hello and firm handshake. Rudy introduces him to Ismene.

John decides not to skirt the issue. "I was with the mayor that morning you and your daughter came to the Clerk's Office. Glad we can meet under more pleasant circumstances tonight."

Ismene nods. "I remember." She appreciates his ability to be up-front and diplomatic at the same time, and continues, "It's not been easy, but we're surviving the public speculation concerning our family. And my daughter is receiving a lesson in what it's like to have life bump up against your ideals." She takes a sip of wine. "Bit of a shock, I dare say."

John, catching the tone of dismay in her voice, tries to reassure her. "It's a rite of passage we all go through, you know. Even so, the older generation always hopes that the next will somehow avoid the tough lessons and tough decisions that follow. But they can't, any more than we could."

Looking past John's shoulder at her daughter who, along with Andrew, is chatting with two people Ismene is certain mean her harm, she confesses, "I fear that, in Annie's case, she will remain starry-eyed at heart—always been a bit different." She gives John a rueful smile. "As a mother I can't help but worry about how she will manage. As a woman, well, perhaps I'm astonished at her ability to identify the best in others no matter what."

John glances behind him to see what she's staring at. "That girl is tougher than you think. I saw how she handled herself after the last Mayor and Council meeting ended. No one can push her around."

Rudy agrees. "There's a lot of you in Annie. She is capable of great strength."

John adds, "That's for certain. We had a very interesting talk, when we met in the library, about giving the dead their due. No matter what the cost is to do so."

"That's my point," Ismene says, eyes still on the four young people in the corner. "She has no sense of self-preservation."

"She has a strong sense of what is right and what is wrong," John replies, "which will see her through."

"And," adds Rudy, "she has your sense of civility. What is true civility except knowing how to be fair?" Rudy is now looking at Andrew, Annie, Robert Greene, and the girl, who's making eyes at his nephew. He firmly adds, "Annie will always be surrounded by people who love her."

THE WAIT-STAFF ANNOUNCES that dinner is served. Robert abruptly takes Lara's arm, and absent his usual love for late entrances, immediately heads to their table, where another five couples will shortly be seated, all cleaved away from Joey Samartino's party and all sharing Robert's desire to see the mayor ousted. Still flushed, he hisses at Lara under his breath, "What was that all about?"

"What?" Lara asks, looking unconcerned.

"I left for a few moments to say hello to some very important people, I turn around, and I find you're talking to, to. . .to *them*."

To check her own rising anger, she inhales deeply, allowing her breasts to rise and fall. Her deep neckline gaps just enough for some black bra lace to peak through.

Momentarily distracted, Robert grabs his scotch and takes a swallow. Breathing hard, he growls, "You're family. Surely, you'd understand—"

"I understand that I *hate* to be left *alone*." Lara gives him a cold smile. "So I went to chat with two new friends, that's all."

"But they're my enemies, for Chrissake."

"*Your* enemies, Robert, not mine. I live in Oklahoma—remember? This networking you do is about *your* connections, *your* future." She dips her index finger into her whiskey and makes a show of tasting it. "Now, if it was *my* future, that would be different."

Robert's eyes suddenly get larger as he grasps her meaning. Feeling cornered, he is about to backpedal his objections when Lara wraps her arm around his neck, her lips barely touching his earlobe. "No one takes me for granted. No one." She exhales a guttural sigh, her warm breath ticking his ear before she sits back in her chair.

She studies the menu that lists the several courses about to be served, letting him sort out his panic and desire. Setting the menu on the table to make eye contact once again, she chuckles as he squirms in his seat. Again she dips her finger into her drink and pouts as she watches the liquid running down the length of it. This time, as she tastes the alcohol, her finger lingers just a bit longer in her mouth. She sees him shudder. Delighted he's no longer able to control himself, commanding his full attention, she exudes an ice-cold indifference. Secretly thrilled at settling the score for his not having called her sooner, she murmurs, "I'm a free agent, so I do what I please, see who I please, whenever I please. Nobody tells me what to do. Least of all you."

Robert remains silent.

Lara frowns to make it quite clear she's not happy with him. "If you don't want me to go to the ICP with *your* enemies, Robert, give me a good reason to make them *my* enemies, too. *Are we clear?*"

Gritting his teeth, he grunts, "Perfectly," and finishes his scotch in one gulp, wondering what kind of sex he will have to perform in order to regain the upper hand in this relationship.

Joey Samartino has just escorted his mother to their table and pulls out her chair. For a week now, Janet's been ill with the flu and suggested that Angela accompany him to the silent auction instead. Joey has always admired his mother's social skills. Though never the life of a party, she's a fully grounded presence exuding real warmth. People sense her kindness and gravitate to her without quite knowing why. She, in return, gives every soul its due.

Though delighted when his mother accepted his invitation, he feels guilty for not having thought of it himself. He's also conscious of not having spent as much time with her as he should, and he makes a mental note to stop by and see her more often.

While she much prefers her own company to an evening of idle chatter, Angela has agreed to join her son in order to see for herself how he behaves with the public. He shares her innate impatience for fools. Eventually, however, she has learned the necessity of compassion when dealing with people—mostly by having observed her husband's deep generosity of spirit toward absolutely everyone. Joey, she suspects, has yet to fully absorb that lesson. And if he is no longer capable of keeping his temper or holding his tongue, he will surely need to reconsider running for office next year.

Therefore, she has taken extra care in dressing for this event. Her thick gray hair is pulled back into a knot at the nape of her neck. A short strand of large pearls that her husband long ago insisted he buy her even though they really didn't have the money for it skims the collar of her black dress and short black jacket, and a set of equally large pearl studs completes the look. Studying her reflection in the mirror earlier in the evening while applying an earth-tone lipstick, her even-handed self-assessment was that, though she's never been a beauty, with the years she's grown into a handsome woman who has managed to maintain that small blessing in old age.

Mother and son are barely settled in their chairs before they hear Christina Hill hail them. "Hello, Angela, my dear, how are you? It's been ages since I saw you last!" She bends down to give her a hug. Looking at Joey, she asks, "Where's Janet?"

Joey rises to receive an enthusiastic hug. "Home, under the weather, so Mom is my date tonight."

"Please give Janet my best, won't you? Sorry to miss her. . . . Can I sit with you for a moment till I join the Clairmonts at their table?"

"Of course," he says, but his attention is immediately drawn elsewhere as a political acquaintance slaps his back and offers him his hand. The women are left sitting by themselves.

"Mrs. Christina," Angela says, admiring the teal swing dress trimmed in sequins that the older woman is wearing. "You are looking very well."

"I feel as fine as I look. Thanks." Christina chuckles, "You call me Mrs. Christina, and I immediately think of Salvatore and his lop-sided grin. It's been, what, two years since he's gone? Tell me, Angela, how are *you* doing?"

"I miss him every day." Angela sighs. "But I keep busy. I see the children and grandchildren when I can, when they can."

Christina is sympathetic. "My nieces' and nephews' lives revolve around *their* kids' sports and social activities. So I play mahjong, see a show in the city as often as I can, and enjoy watching young people move into the neighborhood." She hesitates. "Did you know Ginny Spencer's great-niece moved into her home recently—and the girl's mother, too?"

Angela shakes her head.

"Oh, yes," Christina barrels on. "Such lovely people. They're like family, including me in their lives. . . . Did you, by any chance, hear about the brouhaha about a skull found on Ginny's roof?"

"I read the story." Angela shrugs. "I look at the paper every day. It is one way to find out how my son is doing."

Christina smiles, guessing at everything left unsaid. "Lovely girl, Annie Clairmont. Ginny helped raise her, and in return Annie took care of Ginny during her last weeks. Why, I remember her being a quiet little thing you had to coax a smile from. But once she did, it was magic." Christina sighs. "How time flies."

Angela has begun to understand that there is more to this chance meeting than happy talk. She glances at her son, whose attention remains directed elsewhere, deep in discussion with a couple regarding some political issue. She waits for Christina Hill to make her point.

Christina gives her a half-hearted shrug. "God, it's been decades since that incident. You remember."

Angela waits.

"Annie so wants to clear her family name. She's been asking questions, you see."

"I see." Angela smiles sadly.

"*Do* you?" Christina's public face disappears. A worried look replaces it.

Angela whispers under her breath, "I wondered, too, if the skull is part of the same story. But a promise is a sacred thing, no?"

"I've always thought so, Angela, but Ginny's gone. Don't know about Sylvia. *No* one hears about Sylvia. Still, I can't help asking myself, What about the living? What about this young girl desperate to find out the truth?"

"Secrets!" Angela sips some water. She replaces the glass before looking up. "Mrs. Christina, we do not know if there *is* any connection. For now, all we can do is honor our promise."

". . .Guess so. But secrets have a hell of a way of getting out when you least expect them to."

Angela places her hand on the other woman's shoulder to comfort her. "Very true, my friend. And if it is time for us to tell our story, you and I will know it, and we will do it together."

BY THE END OF THE NIGHT IT HAS BEEN DECIDED that Rudy will return home with Ismene, who was delighted to have won the dinner for four at Mangoire, while Annie will remain to help Andrew clean up after the fête.

As they're dropping extra party favors into a bag, he starts to laugh. She looks up and laughs, too. "I don't know what you find so funny, but you're making *me* laugh. What is it?"

"Oh, I was just thinking about the ICP and the likelihood of the four of us going together. Did you see the look on Robert Greene's face when Lara suggested it? Steam was coming out of his ears." The image makes Andrew chuckle some more as he returns to the business of cleanup and blows out the candles in the votive centerpieces, so the wax will cool enough to handle.

"You mean we aren't going?" asks Annie, disappointed, as she wraps the tiny orange lights into thick coils and lays them in boxes that had been stashed away from view by long tablecloths covering the tables where the gifts were displayed.

"Once I realized that Lara was using me to bludgeon Robert, I simply obliged her. More than one way to skin a cat. Why waste effort going on the offense with him when Lara can take him down all by her lonesome?"

"Hah!" murmurs Annie from under a display table. As she reappears with more light boxes in hand, she adds, "A much more complicated game than I thought. I figured she was just trying to goad me into some reaction."

He smiles. "A woman like Lara makes sure that when she extends her claws to draw blood, no one else is around to witness it. She wouldn't attack you in front of me and risk finding out what I would do to put a stop to it."

Startled, Annie swings around to look at Andrew. But he has his back to her, having grabbed the votives that have cooled, and is searching for the cartons they came it. After slipping them in, he faces her once more, giving her a funny look. "You okay? You've got a very serious look on your face."

She recovers quickly with a grin. "Yes, fine. Just that. . .I liked the idea of going to the ICP, even if it meant going with them."

"I said that the *four* of us won't be going there anytime soon. There's nothing stopping you and me, not even an inconveniently misplaced skull, from doing pleasant things in life. Got anywhere else you'd like to go?"

She thinks about it for a moment. "The Cloisters. I love their gardens, even in the winter."

"Oh, yeah. I forget how great that place is. Haven't been there in years. We'll add it to the list of fun things to do once we solve our 'case.'"

Annie sighs. "You think we ever will?"

"Sure. You know better than almost anyone that secrets don't remain secrets forever. Leave those two big boxes here. Too much to carry all at once. I'll come back for them once everything else is packed."

The cold air of a moonless night is bracing. They stack boxes in the back of his jeep, making sure there's ample room for those remaining in the restaurant. He pushes the back door shut. "I admit I've been dubious all along. But something tells me that we'll get to the bottom of it. Just need to practice a bit of patience. . .hey, did you ever find out anything about that wedding taking place?"

"Oh, I forgot to tell you—after days of scanning old newspapers, I found an engagement announcement dated June 30, 1946, for Winslow 'Buddy' Crocker and Sylvia Elizabeth Ahearn to be wed in July."

"No mention where?"

"Nope. Not part of engagement announcement etiquette."

"I'll have to keep that in mind when I announce my engagement one day."

She shakes her head. "Couples rarely do newspaper *engagement* announcements anymore. It's terribly old-fashioned."

Exhaling, his breath clouds in the cold. Scanning the empty sky, he adds, "Well, I tell you, if anyone ever has the courage to tie the knot with the likes of me, I'd surely announce that miracle in every local paper that exists."

She rolls her eyes. "Oh, please. I watched you circulating tonight. There was no lack of female attention."

He brushed off the observation. "Mostly old friends. Same old same old. Let's say we all know each other too well for any surprises." To change the subject, he asks, "Did you also find the wedding announcement?"

"No. And I looked in all the papers from July to late December, just in case there was some last-minute change. There's no other mention of them again."

CHAPTER 20

PROFESSOR JOHNNY SAMARTINO HAS BEEN TEACHING at a local college for decades. While well-versed in Victorian literature (his specialty) and happy to teach it when he can, he prefers getting into the trenches, helping mostly first-generation freshmen sharpen their ability to think for themselves, and then to write and speak well. Besides being students' tickets to doing well in any profession, he hopes these tools will also help them to become well-informed citizens. As far as Johnny is concerned, literacy insures a stable democracy. His love of books, the English language, and a sense of duty to help others are his father's legacy, and he has practiced it happily all his life. In return for his authentic concern on their behalf, he remains a perennial favorite with the students.

He sits down at a table at the busy Greek luncheonette thirty minutes late because three students stopped him after class with more questions. He tells the awkward young man who is diligently writing down his order that he wants a coffee and pastrami on rye, a gastronomic luxury he allows himself once in a blue moon instead of the boring but healthy garden salad that is his usual choice for lunch. Facing his brother Joey, who already has coffee and a corned beef on rye in front of him and is well acquainted with John's habitual tardiness, he asks, "What's up?"

Startled, Joey replies, "Up? Nothing's up. Can't a guy want to have lunch with his big brother without something being up?"

Giving him a sidelong glance, Johnny smirks. "Usually it's our wives who schedule the get-togethers. Is Mamma okay?" Johnny always refers to their mother in Italian.

"Yeah, yeah. Mom came with me to the Lions' silent auction last night. She's good."

Johnny refrains saying that, in referring to their mother being healthy, he ought to have said 'she is well' instead of what is really a description of her moral character. He sighs and leans back in his chair as Joey continues to speak.

"...Sharp as a tack and physically holding her own. Some reason you're worried about her?"

"She won't listen to reason. I've tried to convince her to move into an apartment, but she refuses to give up the vegetable garden or her roses. I'm concerned about her going up and down those stairs." Johnny throws up his hands in frustration. "Tells me that only when she becomes senile will anyone else make decisions for her, and at that point she won't care anyway. But she's made it quite clear, *she* wants to die at home."

Joey is grateful, as the younger son, that he's been able to duck these discussions. Just imagining the earful Johnny must have gotten, he admires the crazy courage his brother has to pursue this touchy subject out of filial duty. To smooth over the aggravation, he says,

"I'm sure, knowing her, that's exactly how it will happen. She'll be one of those lucky people who dies in bed, in their sleep, simply of old age."

"Which means you and I need to keep a closer eye on her. I can call her in the morning. You, maybe, call her at night?"

"No problem. Besides, I need to stop in and see her more often. Been a bit lax about that."

"Yeah, guilty as charged."

Johnny's order is placed before him. He pauses with his sandwich in mid-air to cautiously ask, "How are things going in town?"

Joey lays down his sandwich, frowning. "Politics are changing. I'm not sure I'm changing fast enough to keep up."

"Mm." Johnny considers this for a moment. "Change is good." Joey gives him a sharp glance, but Johnny waves his hand to head off the usual acerbic remark. "*But* wholesale change is *not*. Better to shake things up with a nod to custom and to experience. Otherwise you're throwing the baby out with the bath water."

". . .I don't think it's the baby they want to throw out," Joey grumbles. "Anyway, it's not something I want to discuss while we eat. But I did want to ask you something about Mom."

". . .Yeah?"

"You remember the first bicycles we ever got?"

"For Christmas?" Johnny asks.

"No, before that."

"Before. . .oh, yeah. That lady Pop did odd jobs for from time to time. What was her name—"

"Spencer."

"That's right! The schoolteacher. Ginny Spencer. Good lemonade, I remember. Mamma liked her a lot."

"Enough, maybe, to keep a secret for over fifty years?"

"Ah, that I wouldn't know. But then again, I wouldn't be surprised either. If Mamma respects you...if she's your friend, you have a fierce ally for life. Why are you asking?"

"I overheard her talking to someone about them keeping a secret for Ginny Spencer all these years."

"News to me. But if Mamma's determined to keep one, neither one of us will change her mind." They ate in silence for a while. "Why do you want to know, anyway?"

"I think it's got something to do with the damn skull they found on the roof."

Johnny whistles. "Now that's some secret!"

LAST NIGHT LARA MADE IT QUITE CLEAR to Robert that he was to keep his hands to himself. If he wants her, he will have to woo her to her satisfaction—and not while spending an evening campaigning for election. All her delicious little ways that he'd become accustomed to were instead spent delighting others at the table. The men couldn't keep their hungry eyes off her. The women, who normally would be staring daggers at her for being a threat, were equally charmed to be in her presence. Her animal magnetism, bordering on the sexual, fueled the attention she aimed at each woman sitting at that table—and gave Robert a moment's pause. And by the end of the evening, everyone at the table had left certain that they were Lara's favorite. Everyone except Robert.

Unlike the frigid weather of the previous night, this evening is unusually mild for early November, yet the smell of burning wood in the fireplace greets him as he rings his Uncle Bob's doorbell. Aunt Elaine hails him with her customary hellos and peck on the cheek, and shows him into the study. She asks if anyone would like a cup of coffee; both men decline, and she shuts the door behind her.

Robert sinks into the chair and faces his uncle. He hates asking for advice, a sign of weakness as far as he's concerned, but there's no one else he trusts.

Uncle Bob gives him a look. "Well?"

"I think, the last time we talked, I didn't follow up with some very obvious questions."

Bob, dreading the continuation of that conversation, gives his nephew a bleak smile. He rests his forearms on the desktop to indicate that he's listening.

"First, I need to know why Lara suddenly shows up. It's been fifty years, as far as I can tell, with no contact between us and the Oklahoma side of the family. But *now* everyone's bending backwards to welcome Lara. It's been—what, nearly nine weeks, and she's stayed with almost everybody except you and Aunt Elaine. Something doesn't add up."

For a moment Bob can't meet his nephews perplexed glance. He rubs his temples. "It rarely does when it comes to guilt."

"Guilt?"

Bob looks up and slowly exhales. "Yes. Guilt. The distance made it easier not to engage, to forget, or tell oneself, 'I'll get to it next week,' until years have gone by and it no longer makes sense to reach out." He drums his fingers on the desk before continuing. "Sylvia was never easy to live with growing up. Lots of mood swings. Sweet one moment, furious the next. And deviousness underscored everything she did. So we learned to give her wide berth."

"But there's forty of us in the family. Whenever we get together, we've pretty much survived on 'live and let live.' What gives?"

"We all have our peculiarities, Robert, no argument there. And we make allowances to keep the peace. Only, Sylvia...Sylvia was in and out of an insane asylum for most of her adult life."

Robert leans back in his chair, mouth open. It takes a while for him to process this. "Was she ever institutionalized here?"

His uncle shakes his head.

"Is that why my mother was livid, hearing that Annie Clairmont was hell-bent on digging up family dirt? She's been in a foul mood ever since."

"Your mother was closest to Sylvia and therefore felt the most betrayed by the absence of *there* there."

"What?" Robert snaps, struggling to understand.

"Off meds, there is no there there. No boundaries exist, no way to get to some negotiated, reasonable outcome that sticks. Yet the meds for someone bi-polar take away the highs as well as the lows. The choices are not great. In the end, the immense distance between Sylvia and the rest of the family made it easy to go on with our lives as if she didn't exist."

It is Robert's turn to be silent. He inspects the stylized floral pattern on the blue oriental under his feet for some time before meeting his uncle's gaze to ask, "Would Ellen's pregnancy have been her way of escaping Aunt Sylvia?"

"Probably, but that's only a guess. Your grandmother kept in touch with Sylvia till her death. But your grandmother never talked about it, and if anyone was foolhardy enough to bring up the subject, she'd start swearing till we all retreated. The subject became taboo."

"Is Sylvia in a hospital now?"

Bob hesitates, feeling his failure to care. ". . .She died this summer. I don't know what kind of arrangements my sister made for her granddaughter. Lara, I assume, using Sylvia's address book, wrote to your grandmother, not knowing she's been gone for years or that your Uncle Richie's now living in the house. We all read her letter asking for a place to stay while she figures out her next step. We decided to open our homes to her for a little while. It was the very least we could do.

"Why all this sudden interest in Lara's past?"

Robert, looking uncomfortable, again doesn't immediately answer.

"I see. You know the old saying, If you have to ask how much it costs, you can't afford it?"

Robert gives him a quizzical look.

"Too many questions surrounding your choice of girlfriend," Bob explains, "probably means it's not a match made in heaven. Either you want someone and you're willing to take on the whole package, or. . . ." He levels a stern look at his nephew to underscore what he's about to say. "Or you walk away like a gentleman. Trick is, Robert my boy, not to confuse sex with love."

Robert meets his uncle's gaze. "She's really beautiful."

"That she is."

". . .And smart."

Bob clears his throat, peering at his nephew over his glasses, and dryly replies, "Depends on whether cunning meets your definition of smart. In that respect, Lara reminds me a bit too much of Sylvia."

Robert considers this for awhile. "There *is* a side to her that scares me."

"Oh? Let me guess—strong willed, maybe? Or demanding—"

"Yeah!" Robert is startled by his uncle's assessment.

"Demanding like. . .your mother, for instance?"

Robert sits back in his chair with a look of horror.

"We all marry our mothers. The difference between a happy and unhappy marriage is which aspect of our mother's personality do we choose to marry. Bossy and capable are not the same thing. Your mother is both. All I can advise you to do now is, *choose wisely.*"

THE NEXT DAY PAUL DEMARIA IS STANDING outside his kitchen door in the cold, clear morning light, stamping his feet to keep warm. The moment he spots Joey making his way to the town hall, he waves to catch his attention. Samartino, in turn, motions for Paul to join him.

For half a block the brown leaves rustling in the wind are the only sound. Joey, having assessed his neighbor's mood, braces himself before asking, "So what's on your mind, Paulie?"

Paul shrugs. "Nothin' that makes me happy."

"Oh?"

"It's like you said, Joey, bad news is something you don't wanna talk about. I mean, even in politics there's a limit, right?"

"There certainly is for me." Joey knocks the ashes from his cigar with a grimace. "One thing I know for sure, I never have and never will run for office on rumor or innuendo."

"Yeah, I'm with you, Joey." They walk in silence for a while.

"But you weren't waiting for me in the cold over nothing."

The other gives him a mournful look. "Well, I got this from a friend of the wife, who happens to be close to Richie Ahearn's wife. She got it on the QT and don't want her name mentioned."

Joey tries to hide his smile. The fastest way to advertise anything is to say it's a secret. "And Richie Ahearn is. . . ?"

"The oldest of the Ahearn clan."

"Ah. And?"

"Sylvia Ahearn's fiancé died the day before the wedding."

"That's sad news, but if I understand correctly, it happened a long time ago."

"Not a story with a happy ending, Joey. In fact, it stinks, if you ask me. It stinks to high heaven." Feeling the cold, Paul turns up his collar and shoves his hands into the pockets of his jacket. "Them rumors I heard were right. Sylvia *was* pregnant. The groom's family, who were there for the wedding, immediately took her and the son's body back to Oklahoma. They wanted to help raise their son's child."

"Honorable." Samartino pauses before asking, "What does it have to do with my campaign, Paulie?"

"I'm not sure," says the other, warming to the story, "but here's what I heard. Sylvia's daughter died giving birth to a baby girl. The father of the little girl got married again, so Sylvia ended up raising that girl—Lara, the one who's hanging around Greene now."

"Oh, yeah. I couldn't help noticing her the other night at the auction. A real looker."

". . . Well, that's just it, Joey."

"What?"

"The part of the story worries me—the part that don't add up. For some reason, Sylvia blamed *Ginny Spencer* for the guy's death, and she kept on blaming her till the day she died."

Joey's brow knits in confusion.

Paul heaves a sigh. "Sylvia Ahearn died in June, and Ginny Spencer in August. Weird, huh?"

"Yeah, but—"

"What if I tell you that Sylvia hated Ginny so much that it pushed her to the point of crazy, so that she was locked up in the loony bin a couple times? And that her cuckoo has rubbed off on the grandkid? Anyway, that's what Richie Ahearn's wife started thinking after Lara spent ten days at their place. The girl makes it quite clear to anyone who will listen that she's got it in for the Spencers, just like her granny did."

"I see." Joey exhales deeply. "...This needs some more follow up."

CHAPTER 21

A FTER A LONG DAY WORKING alongside his staff to begin winterizing client gardens, Rudy Handelman returns home to shower and change into a pair of khakis and a long-sleeved polo shirt. On the spur of the moment, he decides to call upon Ismene, grabs his heavy tan jacket and brown trilby, and marches across the street to knock on the Clairmont door. He's aware of feeling somewhat disloyal to Ginny to now regard this house as anything other than the Spencer home after all these years, but if he knew Ginny at all, she'd think him a fool not to.

A delighted Ismene answers the door and invites him to join her for tea. A brewed pot of lapsang covered by the now familiar cat cozy, a large plate of salmon and cream cheese tea sandwiches, and a second plate piled high with ginger spice cookies are nestled on the tea tray, sitting on the coffee table. As the two of them settle onto the wingback chairs, Rudy is about to ask whether Ismene was expecting guests when they hear Annie bounding down the stairs. As the young woman reaches the last step and turns to make her way into the parlor, she halts, surprised to see a guest *and* the Imari set once again in use. "Oh, sorry. . .I mean, hi, Mr. Handelman. Um, am I interrupting?"

Rudy is accepting a cup filled with steaming tea from Ismene, who retorts, "Don't be ridiculous."

Ismene reaches for the third and last cup on the tray to pour her daughter some tea while Annie makes herself comfortable on the couch barely fast enough to accommodate Alma as she jumps onto the girl's lap. With a pair of tongs, Ismene places two triangles of tea sandwiches on a plate, thinks better of it, and adds one more, tilting it upright against the other two stacked halves, before handing it to Rudy with a shrug.

"I'm remembering more about spending time with Aunt Ginny. I fear some of these memories beg more questions than offers answers."

"What concerns you?" asks Rudy before taking an appreciative bite.

Ismene shrugs again as she hands Annie a plate of sandwiches. "When I was a little girl, Aunt Ginny sometimes babysat me to get me out of my mother's hair while she did the housework. I will confess, sometimes I'd misbehave on purpose so that my mother would, in exasperation, send me here for a few hours. We used to have milky tea and cookies in the kitchen. Aunt Ginny would read to me Grimm's fairy tales. Mother thought them too violent for a little girl to hear. It was our secret, Aunt Ginny's and mine." Ismene smiles as she lays a sandwich on her plate. "Such a lovely memory."

Annie remains silent, having concluded it is wise not to let on that this is a very similar memory to her own when she visited Aunt

Ginny. It's rare for her mother to soften up enough to allow herself the luxury to reminisce, but always worth it.

"Aunt Ginny," continues Ismene, "would set out on the kitchen table a starched pink tablecloth with tiny matching pink napkins embroidered with red roses. Because she never scolded me, I was calm and confident in her presence when she gave me a grown-up china cup and saucer decorated with red cabbage roses." Ismene shakes her head, having smiled as the image came to mind. "There was more milk than tea in the cup, and we ate snickerdoodles, all the while laughing and talking about the stories we read together. We'd have so much fun making up sillier and sillier endings for them. It was magic. Since then, there are few things that make me happier than having tea."

Rudy thinks about a long-held secret he has never shared with anyone. "I ate snickerdoodles and drank tea from the very same teacup and saucer when she tutored me in math. We had tea at the dining room table. My reward for working hard through the math problems I had to complete for homework. And though tea-time was far too close to dinnertime, I'd always push myself to finish supper, even though I was more than full. I never wanted to get in trouble for having enjoyed tea and cookies with your aunt. I was afraid that if my mother found out, she'd put an end to it. So I'd eat all my vegetables without any fuss, making sure no one would ask me why I wasn't hungry that night."

Rudy and Ismene exchange smiles, delighted they have this shared experience.

"Since we're on the subject," she continues, "I now recall an afternoon when it wasn't so magical. . . . I guess I chose to forget it happened." She pours more tea into everyone's cup. "Not surprising, since I don't remember Aunt Ginny ever crying except that one time. And as a kid, I didn't understand what was making her so sad, or even how to make it better."

She puts down her teacup down and squares her shoulders. "Once, while we were together reading a story, a man I didn't recognize came knocking at the kitchen door. Looking back on it now, it seems very probable that person was Buddy Crocker. He came to see her. They went into the parlor and talked for a long time. I got bored and tiptoed as close to the door as I could get without being seen. I could hear Aunt Ginny crying, so I peeked in. The man looked miserable, pacing up and down the room. Finally, he sat on the couch with his head in his hands and said he had to marry "her" now. He had made a promise to "her" long before he really knew her, but now it was the only honorable thing to do, because she was carrying his child. At that moment, they both noticed me. Aunt Ginny got up, wiping her eyes, and told me to go sit in the kitchen and have some cookies, that she'd be in shortly."

"This seems to suggest that your aunt had feelings for someone none of us were aware of," muses Rudy, closing his eyes as he considers this information. "It must have been hard to say good-bye a second time to someone she loved."

Ismene apologizes to her daughter. "You were right to insist on looking into whether or not a wedding took place here. If it was a shotgun wedding, and those who were meant to be together couldn't be, it makes sense that she hid her correspondence with Buddy. . .and no wonder the wedding didn't take place here."

Annie, nodding, scratches the cat behind the ears. "This actually makes a lot of sense. I read through a whole lot of post-World War ll engagement announcements. Most of them appeared in the papers a couple of months before the wedding. Not Sylvia's. It came out the end of June and announced that the wedding was supposed to take place in July. Seemed odd to me at the time, but I figured either the couple was very much in love and couldn't wait. . .or they couldn't wait because Sylvia was pregnant." She glances at Alma contentedly purring like a truck, eyes shut. "Now I know it's the latter."

Rudy, noticing a chill in the air, feels older than he would like to. "I'm not sure this unhappy information gives us the clarity we need. We still don't know where the skull comes from, who it is, or why it ended up here of all places."

"No, we don't," Ismene agrees. "But I bet the two stories are all linked. No two ways about it. . . . Would you like another sandwich, Rudy?"

LATER THAT EVENING, ANGELA SITS at her kitchen table, stone silent, frowning.

"You don't want to help me?" Joey asks, more hurt than surprised.

"You know better than to listen to a private conversation. Unlike your brother who never cared, you always seemed to know when your father and I didn't want you to hear something. That is why we spoke in Italian."

Joey chuckles. "That's how I *learned* Italian, listening to the two of you try to hide information from me. I learned enough to make out what you were saying."

She does not appreciate her son's sense of humor at this moment. And she resents his attempt to force her hand. She considers her options before asking, "And why do you need me to break a promise I made to never betray a secret?"

"Honestly, I'm not sure. But if it helps you decide whether to help me, here's what I know. About fifty years ago, a girl was about to get married when her fiancé died the day before the wedding. She was pregnant. His people, who were from Oklahoma and had traveled here to attend the wedding, left, taking the bride and the groom's body back home. Decades later, the granddaughter shows up, talking trash that her grandmother, who's been in and out of asylum, and is now dead, believed that Ginny Spencer—whose home was recently decorated with an unidentified skull—is to blame for that man's death. Meanwhile, this young woman's cousin is running against me for the party's mayoral nomination. Maybe he's been egged on by the granddaughter's deep resentment for the Spencer family, and maybe not, but he decides it's to his political advantage to make a big deal out of the awkward discovery, insinuating that I'm running scared and not interested in pursuing the truth—even though it's protocol, in such a situation, for the county and state to take over the investigation. But mere facts don't stop rumors from flying."

Still frowning, Angela demands, "And so you are going to behave as mindlessly as they do?"

Unable to keep from raising his voice, Joey responds, "Are you asking if I intend to run a campaign based on rumors? The answer is no."

"So why—"

"—I need *leverage*, Mom, in order to put this right. Greene isn't going to stop without me having some kind of leverage."

"Leverage! Have you become a thug?"

"No," Joey snaps. He looks away to get control of himself before he continues. "Remember your lecture about my living legacy in politics—that I'm supposed to teach my young opponent how to be a *mensch*? How do I do that if he isn't paying attention to anything I say? How do I stop the world for someone more impressed by appearances than substance. . .and get him to *listen*, if I don't have leverage?"

Arms crossed in front of her, she gives the matter some thought. Finally, she concedes, "I understand. But I am not alone in this situation. First, I have to think and be clear about what I am about to do. Then I have to discuss it with others, who are part of this story. You understand, Joey?"

"Yeah, Mom," Joey sighs, suddenly feeling fatigued. "Unfortunately, I do."

"I have a legal question I must ask."

He gives her a surprised look. "Legal? You? I can't imagine you ever doing anything wrong."

"I did no one harm. But what if you heard something that was not a hundred percent right. After so many years, and with everyone involved now dead, am I. . .am I, what is the word—culpable?"

"As a witness? Don't think so. But I can't know for sure until I hear the story."

"Joey, dear, that is the point. What if you hear the story, and my burden becomes yours?"

"Tell her I'm busy."

"Your mother isn't taking no for an answer. She wants to talk to you," Kathy replies in her customary even tone.

Robert silently curses. He picks up the receiver and barks, "What is it you want, Ma?"

"I *want* you to come by for dinner tonight. I haven't seen you for a while. Lara and I are missing your company."

"Yeah, it's just I've been busy at work, meetings, you know."

"Don't give me that crap. I know that you've found time to visit my brother this week. I bumped into Elaine at the supermarket today. But you can't seem to find time to return my calls."

"A legal matter I wanted to run by him."

Harriet lowers her voice, hissing into the phone, "In my opinion, what I see is that at the very least you are shirking your duties to the family by ignoring Lara and leaving me to do all the work of entertaining her. On a bigger scale, you are letting a real catch slip through your fingers. I don't understand it for the life of me, but she's interested in *you*."

"Well, Ma, maybe I'm not so interested in her."

"Are you ever going to get married like a normal person and give me grandchildren, or what?" There is a pause for a moment before she continues. "You're okay, aren't you? I mean you're not in the closet or something, are you?"

Robert rolls his eyes and decides to go on the offensive. "No, I'm not in the closet. No, I'm not ill. No, I'm...I'm not *crazy*, either. At least as far as I know, my genetics in this matter are more from the Greene side of the family, than the Aherns'."

The silence lasts only a few seconds before she screams, "Why you—"

He hangs up on his mother, not waiting to hear the rest of her diatribe.

Although he knows he's going to pay dearly for his actions, it feels good to have the last say. He glances at the work in front of him and sighs, trying to figure out how he can ease himself out of Lara's grip with the least hassle possible to himself. His uncle is right. The Lara he saw that night at the silent auction is not someone he wishes to tango with for a lifetime, no matter how good the packaging looks. Exhaling once more, he drops his shoulders, both relieved and regretful that he's never taken the opportunity to bed her.

The only way to escape is to quickly become involved with someone else. Then the point would be moot. The problem is, there's no one he can think of who fits the bill and is available.

Suddenly he opens his eyes. Maybe that Clairmont girl can be won over. . . . She's not bad looking come to think of it. And this solves two problems: She'll stop attacking him, and Lara and his mother will get off his back. The more he mulls over the possibility, the more appealing the idea becomes.

But the sticking point is that they didn't have a very good start. Robert leans back in his chair to consider this. Finally, he smiles; women *love* men who are sensitive and can apologize for their behavior. That's it. That will do the trick to get her to fall for him. He can be a feeling kinda guy if the occasion requires it. He'll make a big show of saying he's sorry and asking for her forgiveness for his "terrible" behavior. That'll win her over *and* get the two pain-in-the-neck women in his family off his back.

Besides, he's heard the talk that the Clairmonts have money. So in the long run, this mess he finds himself in can be turned into a real opportunity. He marries the rich wife he's hoping for after all.

The more he thinks about this, the more he likes it—definitely a win-win situation. And what woman doesn't love a wild, whirlwind romance that ends in marriage in a matter of weeks? What a great story we'll be able tell people about boy meets girl, boy loses girl, boy comes to his senses and sweeps girl quickly and completely off her feet. And what are the chances she won't be at the next Mayor and Council meeting?

CHAPTER 22

IT IS A CLEAR NOVEMBER DAY, and the setting sun is turning the landscape a deep golden red. This light, Christina's favorite, filters into the living room, where she has prepared a tray with four madeira glasses, nearly filled to the brim, for her company. She offers a glass to each of the three women who have been quietly discussing the weather, before taking the last one for herself. She sighs as she settles into the sofa seat next to Angela. Annie and Ismene, seated in club chairs flanking the sofa on either side, look somewhat expectantly at their hostess.

Christina raises her glass. Everyone else follows suit. "To truth, courage, and the common sense needed for both." She knocks back her drink and watches everyone else politely take a sip. Years of dancing on stage have ingrained the habit of looking confident no matter what, a skill she is thankful she can still muster up in a pinch.

Nevertheless, it takes a moment to for her to begin. "We have talked it over." She glances at Angela, who nods encouragement. "It is one thing to keep silent when no one questions you about something that took place ages ago—and which, at the time, seemed like a good idea. But first you, Annie, and now Angela's son, Joey, have been poking around, asking about the same incident. We decided to tell you what happened being Ginny's close family...and because the story involves her student and her house. It's what we know...but like I always say, who the hell really knows another person's heart?"

Resting a hand on Christina's arm, Angela murmurs, "I think perhaps I'd better say what I know first. During the last years of the war, my husband decided to make extra money for my sons to go to college one day. Mrs. Christina introduced him to Miss Ginny. She hired him to do some work around her house." Angela meets Ismene's unsettled look straight on and smiles. "When my boys and I brought him lunch, I saw she was a good woman. I liked her very much."

Ismene opens her mouth to speak, thinks better of it, and instead rearranges herself on her chair.

Angela continues. "Salvatore was to clean out the leaves in the gutters one Sunday morning. He showed Miss Ginny that one of the top steps of her ladder was cracked. She said she would go buy a new one right away. My husband said he could work around it, but, sooner or later, she would need a new one, so no one got hurt. There was a young girl with Miss Ginny that day who heard them talking. Salvatore later told me it was the same girl who was to be married in Miss Ginny's house."

At this point, Christina takes up the story. "Angela is talking about Ginny's pupil, Sylvia Ahearn. The bride and groom didn't have much money, so Ginny offered her home for the ceremony. We all pitched in to help her and the couple with the wedding preparations." Christina glances at Annie, who has not said a word so far, but who reaches for some chocolate-covered coffee beans from the little dish on the coffee table and places one in her mouth.

"It was different then. Weddings were simple. In some ways, they were far more joyful than the elaborate affairs that happen today. Angela had baked a huge cake. I provided the champagne as a gift to the couple. Ginny prepared the canapes. Everything was being set up to allow guests, after the ceremony finished in the parlor, to mill around the garden, eat a few deviled eggs, toast the happy couple, have a piece of cake, and call it a day." She shakes her head before resuming the story.

"On the day before the wedding, Angela and I were in the kitchen, washing and drying the champagne glasses. Ginny was at the breakfront in the dining room, pulling out plates for the appetizers and bringing them into the kitchen for a wash. Sylvia had set up the ironing board in the hallway to press the linens.

"Ginny had just finished arranging flowers for the vase that sat on the hallway table. She told Sylvia that she'd decided not to wait for Salvatore to hang the white streamers from the oak tree.

"As Ginny pulled out the ladder to set it against the tree, I accidentally broke one the champagne glasses and got cut between my thumb and forefinger. Ginny hurried into the kitchen to look at it, having been well trained by her father in such matters, and made sure the gash stopped bleeding. I felt like a fool, insisting that I pay to replace the broken glass. Ginny wouldn't hear of it. She disappeared from the kitchen into the dining room, rummaged through the breakfront, found four more champagne glasses, and set them down on the kitchen table, saying, 'Here, just in case we need extra.'

"As she went outside to finish her work and was about to get on the ladder, Buddy stopped by to see if we needed help. He insisted on hanging the crepe streamers himself. . .and as he reached the top of the ladder, a rung broke. He fell backwards and came crashing down onto the ground." Christina stares at her hands folded on her lap. "It was awful. He didn't move. Ginny yelled out for us to call for an ambulance. We all came running, including Sylvia, who started screaming. Ginny tried to calm her down, but the girl got more and more hysterical, striking out at Ginny, trying to scratch her eyes out."

Angela, agitated by the memory, says, "My husband also was coming by to help move tables and chairs. He heard screaming and ran to the backyard. He pulled the girl away, holding her tight in his arms, but she kept shouting how she hated Miss Ginny and struggled to get free of his grip.

"It was a terrible scene. The young man's body lying on the ground, and the girl howling, 'It was you, *you* who were supposed to die, not Buddy! *Now* who is going to take care of me and my baby?' By the time the police and the ambulance came, Sylvia was in a chair, holding her head and moaning. When the police questioned Miss Ginny, who was the only one to see the accident happen, she did not tell them what the girl said. None of us did."

Angela closes her eyes and sighs, "Miss Ginny was too kind a woman to think anything bad about Sylvia. She believed the girl was out of her mind with grief and saying things that made no sense.

"They told us that Buddy broke his neck and was dead. The ambulance took the body away. After that, Miss Ginny called his family, who were staying at a hotel, to tell them what happened. She also called Sylvia's family to come get her and take care of her, because nothing we could do helped. When everyone else left, Salvatore and I stayed to look after Miss Ginny. She looked as pale as a ghost. I made her some tea. My husband took a good look at the broken ladder. It was the old one with the cracked step, the one that Miss Ginny hadn't gotten around to throwing out yet. It had been lying on the side of her garage for months, waiting for her to leave it at the curb on the correct trash day. This made him suspicious, because for many months, when he did work around Miss Ginny's house, he was using the new ladder she had bought. He decided to look for it and started searching for it in the garage, since the garage door was, as usual, left open. It didn't take him long to find it shoved out of sight under Miss Ginny's car.

"The next day, Mrs. Christina, my husband, and I went to see how Miss Ginny was doing. We learned Buddy's parents were leaving immediately, taking their dead son to Oklahoma to be buried on the farm in the family cemetery, and taking Sylvia with them. The four of us agreed to never speak about what the girl had said. What good could come of demanding justice in this sad affair with an unborn baby already fatherless?"

Nothing is said for a long while, until Annie, looking at no one in particular, asks, "Did Aunt Ginny blame herself?"

Christina, who considered Ginny a close friend, replies, "If you mean whipping herself with could of, would of, should of—no, she was made of sterner stuff. But she wasn't the same after Buddy died. I mean, she was all of twenty-seven when it happened, but never again did she show the slightest interest in dating, let alone getting married. It was as if she had decided to live as a monk, devoting her life to others. I've always wondered whether she chose to live that way as penance."

Angela knew hunger as a child and saw the terrible things it did to the human heart—how envy, suspicion, and hatred kept some people in her village alive when there was little else. It eventually destroyed them—and very often their families with them. She reaches over to take Annie's hand in hers. "I believe your aunt finally saw the young woman who meant her harm as she really was. No person faces such hatred without being changed forever. It is like a wall of fire with no beginning or end that destroys whatever it can to stay alive. But...in the end, it is the person who hates who burns up completely and turns to ash, into the living dead. This your aunt would not soon forget."

"No wonder," Ismene murmurs, "as I was growing up, I always found the house and my aunt a little sad. Choosing to be alone must have been hard." She reaches for her glass of madeira and takes a sip. To change the subject, she asks, "Angela, why is your son interested in this story?"

"Those who attack your family's reputation do so to come after my son politically. It is easy enough to say the enemy of my enemy is my friend. But I think there has been enough bad blood for more than one lifetime. This must stop."

Annie looks at her quizzically. "You mean a happy ending after all?"

"A better ending, perhaps."

Ismene gives this some thought. "What is it you need from us, Angela?"

"Permission to tell my son the full story."

Ismene shakes her head. "To go public with it. Oh, I don't think so. Poor Aunt Ginny deserves some peace. . .some shred of dignity left. Look, as much as I would love to help you out—"

"No, no, not to shame anyone publicly. I would not stand for that. Neither would my son. He already knows most of the story. Everything except what was in that girl's heart—to do harm to another human being. But he would want the story to put an end to these terrible lies once and for all. I ask, as Ginny's closest living relatives, that you release me from my promise."

Annie, showing some newfound political forethought meets her mother's eyes. "As you well know, no secret stays secret forever. Better we control this piece of news than wait around and let it control us. I say we ask Mayor Samartino to join us for some madeira."

CHAPTER 23

ROBERT'S GOOD MOOD AS HE HURRIES toward the municipal building fizzles when he spies his mother and Lara waiting at the door. He immediately smiles. "Well, well, well," he says as he approaches them, "what a surprise. What brings you here tonight?"

Lara, matching his cheerfulness note for note, answers, "Why, you, of course." In a very short sweater skimming the top of black leggings that seem to have been poured onto her body, she's in profile, so the curves of her behind are shown to their advantage. "We haven't seen you in ages. . .so here we are. The mountain has come to Mohammed."

The muskiness of her perfume greets him from several feet away. To hide his altered feelings, he gives her body a long, appreciative look.

His mother waits, watching him hungrily eye the bait, and is pleased. She says with uncharacteristic graciousness, "Shouldn't a mother have the pleasure of seeing her son doing well in the public eye? It's about time I came to one of these meetings and watched you work."

The three enter the council room and take their seats. Usually, he'd be pleased by so much attention. But his mother isn't capable of thinking of anyone else in any sustained fashion, and Lara is an expensive indulgence he is longer considering seriously. While the two could cramp his style tonight, he will try instead to use their bothersome presence to his advantage.

For he now fancies himself a knight of the Round Table filled with courage that can only come from the pursuit of true love. He will prove his worth to the modest but beautiful noblewoman—in this case, Annie Clairmont. To win her hand, he will not only apologize for his errant ways on bent knee but spurn the licentious advances of the vixen, Lara Snow. And once he attains Annie's devotion, he will in that union of magical bliss become more like his uncle— a man of probity, a humble but wise servant of the people. Robert settles in and waits for the sound of the gavel.

Joey has been surveying the audience from his seat on the dais. On one side of the room, his mother is with the Clairmont women and their extended entourage, including Christina Hill, Rudy Handelman, and his nephew Andrew. And on the other side, Robert Greene seems to have his family in tow as well. Up front in the first row sits the reporter for the local paper, covering her beat. Joey smiles to himself, cups the mike, and mumbles to Councilman Eddie Polansky, "Are you sure about this?"

"Yeah, boss. It's time, don't you think?"

Joey shrugs. "Not for me to say."

John Kelly slips into his seat, sees Joey's hand still on the mike, and whispers, " I talked to an old friend in the prosecutor's office. Strictly hypothetical, not a problem."

Joey nods, raises and drops the gavel twice to bring the meeting to order. The first thing on the agenda is the parking ordinance, which was introduced at the last meeting and is up for final consideration before a vote. The meeting is opened to the public. Mr. Theodore Blauvelt, with his carved walking stick, slowly makes his way to the microphone and clears his throat before addressing the Mayor and Council.

"I object to this ordinance being adopted." He rumbles on, clearly discontented with the way this century is drawing to its close—in which cars matter more than people do. "But I suspect that my objection is for naught. If this confounded measure must go through, I want to know if the stickers we taxpayers will be forced to pay for will be carefully priced so as not to add insult to injury."

"As always," Eddie answers, "we take at least three bids before giving anyone a municipal contract. John, our town administrator, also speaks with other municipalities that have already introduced similar measures for their feedback on having worked with venders, and whether they have any gripes or recommendations. Anyway, there will be no processing fee involved—you just fill out an application and provide a copy of your car registration."

Satisfied that the Mayor and Council may still have a shred of common sense left, Mr. Blauvelt clears his throat once more and takes his time returning to his seat. Not a sound can be heard in the room, until he settles himself to his satisfaction.

Ismene marches up to the mike, "Ismene Clairmont, 333 Walnut Street. If my car is parked on my street, and I keep it there from 9 a.m. until 11:30 a.m. and I don't have a sticker, would I get ticketed?"

"Not until one minute after 11 p.m. could you receive a parking ticket," Joey answers. "This ordinance is meant to keep people from out of town parking their cars around 8:00 a.m., getting on a bus to go to work, and then returning by bus at 6:00 p.m. to pick up their cars and go home. In fact, we are one of the last towns on bus routes into the city to adopt such a measure."

"What about out-of-town guests?"

"They can come to the municipal building and get a guest pass for the duration of their visit."

Satisfied, Ismene returns to her seat.

Margie whispers to Annie, "You think you-know-who is going to get up and speak?"

"As sure as the sun rises in the east," Annie replies, looking over her shoulder to find Robert up and adjusting his suit jacket as he makes his way to the front of the room.

Robert leans into the microphone. "Robert T. Greene, 275 Pine Street. I'd like to ask if the Mayor and Council have explored other avenues? There must be *some* way to avoid inconveniencing the residents as much as this will."

Eddie glances at the mayor, and Joey takes over the discussion. "We looked at different options and chose the least restrictive one— that you can't park on our streets during weekdays for more than two hours from nine in the morning till noon without a resident sticker. We thought this would be both the easiest on residents and the most advantageous choice for businesses in town."

Robert turns and gestures at the audience, making eye contact with his mother, who grins as she returns his look. "But the onus remains on the residents. As Mr. Blauvelt pointed out in the last meeting, it is a real inconvenience."

"Which is why our residential stickers for cars will be valid for three years. You may have noticed—and if you haven't, in most other municipalities where resident stickers exist, they expire after two years."

"Yes, but your ordinance will make it difficult for those who don't have a garage and must park on the street because they have no other choice. In fact, this ordinance will most adversely affect those who live in apartments."

Joey keeps his voice even. "That is not our intention."

"Perhaps not, but it is the final effect, whatever else this ordinance might accomplish in view of the overdevelopment that is taking over our town." With that last swipe, Robert returns to his seat, pleased with how the encounter with the mayor went.

With no other comments coming from the public, the open portion of the meeting closes. Eddie Polansky motions, and Chick Accardi seconds the motion, that the ordinance be voted on. It passes unanimously.

The rest of the agenda goes by quickly and before long Joey bangs the gavel twice and brings the meeting to an end. The reporter ambles up to the mayor, making a point of *not* having her pen poised to write in her notebook when she asks, "You haven't yet declared whether or not you're running for mayor next year."

Joey jokes, "What else am I going to do on Monday and Tuesday nights if I'm not here for the Council or the Planning Board? Life would suddenly get very dull, don't you think?"

She laughs. "Oh, I don't know. I could think of a couple of other ways to spend the time. After all these years—aren't you bored doing the same thing over and over again?"

"Are you?"

"No, but what fascinates me is people's character. You get to see what makes them tick."

"Well, speaking of character, I remember the first Mayor and Council meeting you attended. You stuck out a budget meeting even though it was clear you were lost trying to follow it."

"...You remember that? It must be, what, seventeen years ago." She flashes a grateful smile. "After that meeting ended, you called me up to the dais to show me a line item in the budget—garbage collection. The entry next to it was $95,000.

"First, you explained how the town used to get that $95,000 from the county, which got it from the state, which got it from federal revenue sharing. But national public opinion had veered toward demanding smaller government and lower federal taxes, and the result was you guys in municipal government were forced to raise homeowners' taxes or find that money either by holding down wages and benefits or cutting services—which means people lose jobs."

He nods. "And I remember that you caught on quick when you realized that the lifeblood of town politics was ratables."

She reopens her notebook. "Mr. Mayor, will you be making an announcement about running next year anytime soon?"

She gets a big grin. "I'll give you a heads-up when I do."

"Councilman Polansky told me that he won't be running for reelection next year."

"Yeah, I'm going to miss him. But his heart is in working with kids as a coach, so I understand."

"Got a replacement?"

"Not yet."

They part when one of the residents asks Joey how he can get a side yard variance for his plans to enlarge his kitchen.

Having obtained the appropriate quote from Councilman Polansky regarding parking, the reporter makes her way to Robert to ask follow-up questions about the new ordinance and about next week's Planning Board meeting on the De Vries property. He tells her why he's concerned about overdevelopment but remains noncommittal on the upcoming project. "I'll have to give the entire thing close consideration," he says, "to determine what option would best serve the town."

She flips her notebook closed and takes her leave. Lara, giving Robert a puzzled look, exclaims, "My goodness, if I didn't know better, I'd say you had an off night. You didn't go after the mayor at all."

"I made my point."

"But not a word about the skull. Don't tell me you've lost your nerve, just because the Clairmonts are here."

"I haven't lost my nerve. In fact, I've found it. If you will excuse me." He heads in Annie Clairmont's direction, leaving Lara alone—her aunt is off in the corner, talking to an old friend—and stunned.

"Miss Clairmont—oh, Miss Clairmont, may I speak with you a moment, please?"

Annie has spotted him trotting in her direction. Exhaling, she readies herself for battle but is thrown off guard when he murmurs, "May I speak with you privately?"

She nods, and they walk to the back of the room.

"I must confess, I've taken a good look at myself since the last time we talked—"

"Talked?"

"Well, perhaps 'talked' is not *quite* right. More accurate to say since the dressing down you gave me after the last Council meeting."

"Oh." She blushes. "That—"

He puts one hand up. He notices how pretty she looks flushed with embarrassment and redoubles his efforts. "Before you say another word, I want to tell you that I deserved it. And I feel terrible for running out on you like a coward."

Her eyes grow wide with surprise, and Robert rushes on with his speech. "You were one hundred percent right. I had to ask myself what kind of a politician do I want to be? And should that be any different from the man I choose to be?"

Neither is aware that at least six pairs of eyes are now trained on them as most of the public has emptied out of the council chamber into the small courtyard outside the municipal building.

Margie, watching her cousin and Robert in their huddle, turns to Andrew standing beside her and mumbles under her breath, "You think she needs help?"

He shakes his head. "She can handle him."

"Aren't you. . .concerned?"

"For him, not her. She's very much her mother's daughter and *more* than capable of giving what for. I've had a taste of that temper of hers, you know."

Now it's Margie's turn to shake her head. "Uh-uh," she murmurs, "not what I'm picking up. That's *not* the stance of a man ready to wrestle an opponent."

Andrew glances quickly. Rubbing his chin, he gives some thought to his reply before speaking. "She's capable of fighting her own battles. . .and making up her own mind about what she wants."

"Admirable sentiments," replies Margie with a wry smile, "but I don't see *you* wandering off to chat with anyone else."

He shrugs. Arms folded, shifting his weight to one hip, he keeps watch from a distance.

Robert can see that Annie hasn't yet gotten his drift and tries again. "What I'm trying to say is that I will no longer be bringing up the skull as a political issue. And I should never have done it in the first place. I'm truly *very* sorry for my behavior. Will you please forgive me?"

This is not what Annie expected to hear. But it doesn't take her long to make up her mind. "I accept your apology. And I'm relieved to know that you've decided to drop your smear campaign."

She is about to offer him her hand and then walk away to join her family when he continues, "I never meant to hurt you, and I am distressed if I did so. On the contrary, I have a great deal of respect for you, dare I say—" he smiles as he finishes his speech— "an admiration for your forthrightness and honesty. I could learn a thing or two from you if you let me."

Her eyes widen once more as she begins to understand and starts to back away. "Oh, no, no, that isn't possible. I mean, who am I to teach anyone, well, anything of consequence—really." She inches toward Margie and Andrew, who now seem miles away.

He chuckles, taking a step closer to her as he whispers, "You are always the perfect lady, so unfailingly modest. But I remember the firebrand I met that night I was campaigning on your block. You just wouldn't let anyone push you around."

He lowers his voice to a more intimate tone and adds, "I bet that passion fuels everything you do."

Annie's jaw drops. Before she can respond, Lara lunges at Robert, her hands grabbing fistfuls of his hair and ramming his head against the wall. He yanks himself free as she screams, "You're dumping me for *her*?" She gasps as she tries kicking him in the shin with her high-heeled boot, which he deftly avoids. "*Her* of all people! You ungrateful creep. After all I've done for you. Where would your campaign be if I hadn't thrown Grandpap's skull on that roof?"

Dead silence suddenly blankets the room. Everyone is frozen in place except for Harriet, who makes a beeline for the door.

"Okay," Joey growls, still standing on the dais, taking command of the situation to make sure that this doesn't end up going public. He points to Robert, Lara, and Annie and barks, "You three—into the conference room—now." Then he signals to his mother, Christina, and Ismene to join him, too, in the room the Council uses for closed sessions involving personnel issues that are not privy to the public.

No one says a word as the mayor seats himself at the head of the conference table, while John Kelly takes the chair at the opposite end.

Leveling a look at Lara, Joey asks, "You want to explain yourself?"

Her jaw tenses, but she remains silent and stares out the window.

He raises both hands in a shrug and, addressing the borough clerk, says, "It's a preposterous idea. I mean, think about it. A woman digs up a grave, steals someone's skull, travels halfway across the country, and throws it on a stranger's roof. Come on."

"Hmm." John leans forward to place his chin in his palm to give this some thought. "A grave's what, six by three by eight feet. That's a *lot* of digging for anyone to do, let alone a woman."

Joey leans back in his conference chair, bracing his foot against the leg of the table, before he speaks. "Leaving aside the question of whether a woman has the strength to single-handedly dig up a grave . . . ." He notices Lara smoldering and presses the point further: "What about having the nerve to get on a plane and risk having Grandpap's head being accidentally discovered?"

Robert suddenly snaps to attention. Making eye contact with the mayor, he grumbles, "She didn't take a plane. She came by train."

Lara gives him a dirty look but remains closed mouthed.

"Okay, makes about as much sense as anything does in this story. If you're carrying your own bags onto a train, there's less of a chance of someone else touching them," Joey agrees. "But how do you sneak a skull onto someone's roof?"

Annie clears her throat. "I can answer that. There's a huge oak in the backyard. One of the really big branches is so close to the house that as kids, we used to sneak out the attic window and climb down into the yard."

Ismene stares at her daughter.

"Margie and I would dare each other to do it."

"It's a miracle neither one of you got killed," Ismene snaps. "That's it. Tomorrow morning, pronto, I'm getting someone in to trim that tree."

There's a knock at the door. Poking his head into the room,

Bob Ahearn asks, "Mind if I join you? My sister called me in a panic . . .perhaps I can be of help."

Joey, who knows the judge by reputation, waves him in, and Bob takes a seat next to his great-niece.

Lara finally glares at Joey. "I grew up on a farm. We know what physical work is."

"Oh, for God sake," Ismene says, having lost her patience. "Why on Earth did you do this?"

"Because," Lara practically hisses, "Ginny Spencer killed my grandfather, and my grandmother always wanted *justice*."

"Except that isn't what *happened*!" shouts Ismene, unable to keep her voice from matching the volume of the girl's. "Even though everyone who was directly involved in the incident is dead, we have two witnesses sitting here who can attest to what *did* happen. It was an accident, and it happened because your grandmother secretly switched a broken ladder for a sound one."

"You're *lying*," screams Lara.

"*That's* rich," Ismene screams back, "coming from a woman who dug up her grandfather's head and tossed it onto our roof and then— and then pretended that she didn't know a thing about it, and kept encouraging this *idiot* to slander *my family*." The outraged look she gives Robert prompts him to sink further down in his seat. "And if I have to get a lawyer—"

"No one," Bob murmurs, "wins when lawyers get involved. I can assure you of that."

"No," Annie says quietly. "That won't be necessary." She gives John a wink. He winks back. "This is not about you, me, Robert, or even Lara. This is about making Buddy Crocker, Ginny Spencer, and Sylvia Ahearn whole again.

"Robert, to his credit," she continues, "told me tonight that he no longer intends to pursue the skull story for political gain." She smiles encouragingly at the young man hunched over in his chair who looks up to meet her gaze. "And I believe him."

She turns to Lara, and continues, "Sylvia approached my great-aunt to get tutored to become more ladylike. It took a lot of courage and gumption on your grandmother's part to get up the nerve to ask for that kind of help. It says a lot about her to want to do it. . .and to achieve it. But she wasn't getting tutored in algebra or English. And on some level, to ask for that kind of help must have made her . . .made her angry about not feeling she was good enough. So it would have been natural that Sylvia's feelings toward Ginny were complicated. . .*and* that jealousy and resentment were part of the mix.

"We'll never know the whole story." Annie glances at Christina. "You can never really know another person's heart, but I can say with certainty that my great-aunt wanted to see Buddy and Sylvia married and that is why she offered her home for their wedding."

Only Christina Hill and John Kelly are not surprised by the young woman's compassion. Christina points out, "I know how fond of Sylvia Ginny was. And what a terrible shock for her to realize that Sylvia wanted her dead."

"You cannot change the past," Angela says, giving her son a look. "But you can make up your mind to shape the future."

Joey gives his mother one of his wicked grins. "If I understand you," he asks Annie, "you and your mother are not going to pursue any misdemeanor charges?"

Annie turns to see no objection on her mother's part. "Correct—with the condition that the skull, and our family, will no longer be used as a political bludgeon."

"I can assure you of that," Bob says in a firm and even voice, eyeing his nephew across the table. "I'm relieved to hear Robert has already given his word. But in view of the current situation, he will also immediately withdraw from campaigning for mayor."

Robert is about to object when his uncle gives him a look that means the decision is not up for discussion.

"Well, then, this is good news for me," says Joey, chuckling. ". . . And as it happens, we anticipate having an opening on the Council. So, Robert, how about becoming my running mate next year?"

The young man looks up, but no words come out.

"This way, you don't appear to be backing down from a fight. Instead, you show your willingness to work up the political ladder. If you accept, and we run and win, I will teach you what I've learned in twenty years of politics. And, since you represent the future, you can show me a few things, too. Interested?"

Robert can't believe his ears. "Are you serious?"

"I am. Whaddaya say?"

Robert glances at his uncle who nods imperceptibly. "Sure. It's . . .it's a very generous offer." Robert grabs Joey's hand and adds, "Thanks."

Bob shifts in his chair to face Lara, wearing his best hanging judge look. "My niece will be returning home shortly. I will call her family to explain the situation. I'm sure appropriate arrangements will be made for her, and her grandfather's skull, once they return home. This is the best outcome, given the situation, and the only way I can assure an immediate end to any mischief directed at the Clairmont family."

ANDREW PUSHES OPEN THE WOODEN DOOR at the Cloisters that leads out into a small garden that faces the Palisades rising on the Jersey side of the Hudson River. Annie runs out to inspect the four quince trees, now leafless, standing guard over medicinal or magical herbs gone to seed that circle them in quadrants.

"I can never decide which season I like best being here," says Andrew as he leans over to read about the mandrake, considered during the Middle Ages to be a powerful plant because the root is shaped like a human, but is also poisonous to them.

"I think it's the combination of things that makes this place powerful," she says, strolling to edge of the garden to study the river. "Imagine, for centuries, how many people used these rooms to meditate or to pray in, before the rooms were dismantled and brought here. Or how many people handled the objects of worship before they ended up behind glass. I think these old walls are infused with the best we have to offer—the whole kit and caboodle—our fears, hopes, dreams, and wonder."

He joins her at the stone wall. "You're in a rather philosophical mood."

She giggles. "Can't help it. My imagination runs wild in this place. I see the sarcophagus of a Crusader and can't help but get the feeling I'm looking at an old friend."

"Drifting into past lives, are you?"

She shakes her head. "Not really." She slips her arm around his waist. "This life is just fine. Tonight I meet Jack and Rachel for dinner to get the once-over."

"You're not nervous, are you," Andrew asks as he pulls her near for a kiss.

"A little. What if he really doesn't like me? That would be awkward, since come this Monday, Jack and I will be working in the same building."

"What!"

"It came as a surprise to me, too. John Kelly asked me to meet with him in his office and offered me a job as his assistant. His purpose, which is on the QT, is to train me to eventually take over his job. He says I have the gumption and the heart needed to do the work—help people find their way."

"That's wonderful. Congratulations."

There isn't a living soul in the garden with them when they take their first kiss.

About the Author

Eugenia Koukounas has degrees in both politics and nursing, has had a background in journalism, and writes both nonfiction and fiction. She has studied and practiced Taiji, Kabbalah, and Shamanism for many years and now teaches Kabbalah through bluerosesandpine.com. She is currently at work on her third Kabbalistic volume, a synthesis of Eastern and Western spiritual disciplines. She lives with her husband, the novelist and poet Barry Sheinkopf, in Northern New Jersey.

CPSIA information can be obtained
at www.ICGtesting.com
Printed in the USA
BVHW052219120922
646875BV00003B/139